D1736632

Love is
a time of enchantment:
in it all days are fair and all fields
green. Youth is blest by it,
old age made benign:
the eyes of love see
roses blooming in December,
and sunshine through rain. Verily
is the time of true-love
a time of enchantment — and
Oh! how eager is woman
to be bewitched!

THE TOAST OF THE TOWN

Beautiful and coltish Georgiana Eversley was well aware of her intoxicating powers. She took it for granted that she could captivate any man who caught her fancy, though few men did. But when the handsome Dr. John Graham let it be known that he didn't care for her at all, Georgiana's hurt pride demanded revenge. And so it was that she accepted a daring wager to prove that she could indeed entice the young doctor and jilt him savagely as well. But Georgiana was unaware of the whims of passion . . .

Books by Alice Chetwynd Ley
Published by The House of Ulverscroft:

THE JEWELLED SNUFF BOX
A CONFORMABLE WIFE
THE GEORGIAN RAKE
THE MASTER OF LIVERSEDGE
AT DARK OF THE MOON
MASQUERADE OF VENGEANCE
TENANT OF CHESDENE MANOR

ALICE CHETWYND LEY

◆

THE TOAST
OF THE TOWN

Complete and Unabridged

ULVERSCROFT
Leicester

First published in Great Britain

First Large Print Edition
published 1998

British Library CIP Data

Ley, Alice Chetwynd, *1913 –*
The toast of the town.—Large print ed.—
Ulverscroft large print series: romance
1. Romantic suspense novels
2. Large type books
I. Title
823.9′14 [F]

ISBN 0–7089–3884–1   00-804704

Published by
F. A. Thorpe (Publishing) Ltd.
Anstey, Leicestershire

Set by Words & Graphics Ltd.
Anstey, Leicestershire
Printed and bound in Great Britain by
T. J. International Ltd., Padstow, Cornwall

This book is printed on acid-free paper

To our
dear Helen Diana

1

Angry Young Man

DARKNESS had fallen, and the watchman had already started on his rounds; but judging by the commotion in Curzon Street, it might still have been broad daylight. There was a constant clatter of wheels and hoofs as carriage after carriage passed over the uneven cobbles. Link boys ran here and there carrying flares to light the chairmen, who jostled each other and exchanged rough jests in a strong Irish brogue as they plodded along bearing their elegant burdens.

Outside my lord Eversley's house, which was ablaze with light, the vehicles and sedan chairs halted to discharge occupants attired for the most part in the first style of fashion. The visitors made their way up the red-carpeted steps to the bright, welcoming interior of the house, where footmen resplendent in handsome blue livery waited to announce them in sonorous tones to Viscount Eversley and his family.

"My lord Pamyngton!" intoned a footman. "My lord Curtoise and Miss Waverley! Mr. Sheridan!"

Richard Brinsley Sheridan, renowned alike as a politician and a playwright, advanced towards his hosts to make his bow. As he did so, he took stock of them with the keen eye that had observed and noted so many of the follies and foibles of his day.

He had often enough heard them called the irresistible Eversleys. Well, there was some truth in it, he acknowledged, seeing them all standing together. They were a strikingly handsome family, with their arresting tawny hair and almost classical cast of features. The eldest son, Hugh — known to the Town as Beau Eversley — had the advantage of his two brothers in height, and also in elegance of manner. The middle one, George, was more stockily built, and had the look of a sportsman. Close to his side was the pale, mousy little girl to whom he had recently become betrothed. What a fool the chit was, reflected Sheridan, to stand next to Viscount Eversley's younger daughter, Georgiana!

For Georgiana Eversley was undoubtedly the kind of female whom men looked at twice, and then again as often and as lingeringly as opportunity permitted. It was not so much that she was an uncommonly handsome female, either, the playwright decided with unerring perception. Her real attraction lay in the sheer vitality of her, which shone from her exciting green eyes, and showed in every slightest movement of her supple body.

His glance passed reluctantly from Georgiana to her elder sister Evelina, whose married name was Cunningham and in whom traces of the same allure lingered. Last of the Eversley brood was Frederick, a young man of nineteen who gave promise of being his brother Hugh all over again.

There was someone missing, though, thought Sheridan with a slight frown. Yes, of course, it was Beau Eversley's wife, the dark little female with the elfin face and big, dreamy eyes that so patiently worshipped her husband.

His glance ranged about, and eventually discovered Susan Eversley sitting close by among a group of dowagers. He smiled; the little creature could manage to look pretty even when she was breeding, it seemed. She was really very like her Mama, the spirited Maria. He must go and pay his respects. Yes, undoubtedly the Eversleys were an interesting family, and with a streak of wildness — if all accounts were true — which was not unexpected in people with hair of that colour. Material for a play? He smiled to himself, remembering the success of 'The School for Scandal' and of his more recent, though very different production 'Pizarro'. One never knew; sometimes material would lie dormant in the creative mind for years, before bursting into urgent life. Time would show.

After Mr. Sheridan had made his bow to Susan and passed on to join a group of other acquaintances, Georgiana Eversley came over to her sister-in-law and slipped into a vacant chair beside her.

"I fear this is going to be a vastly tedious affair," she whispered in Susan's

4

ear. "I am bored to death already, and I'm sure you must be, in such company."

She flashed a look at the group of dowagers gathered round Susan, and made a wry face. She particularly disliked the small, sharp-featured lady who sat on Susan's other side. This was Mrs. Curshawe, mother of George's betrothed, and well known for her acid tongue.

"Nothing of the kind!" returned Susan, with a laugh. "I have been having a most entertaining conversation with Mr. Sheridan. He is one of the few people, you know," she added, lowering her voice, "to whom I can speak of my mother, for naturally he knows her as an actress."

"Well, let us hope that your neighbour didn't hear you at it," said Georgiana, "or it will be all over Town by morning! Really, Sue, can you imagine whatever George can possibly see in that insipid Caroline Curshawe? I dare swear she never says or does anything that Mama hasn't first approved — and just imagine how that limits the possibilities!"

"She is only eighteen," whispered Susan, with a guilty look in Mrs.

Curshawe's direction.

"If she lives to be eighty, she'll never be anything but a dead bore," asserted Georgiana. "Her brother's just the same — and believe it or not, Sue, Hugh's been such a muttonhead as to ask all three of them to join us at Fulmer Towers next month! I declare I think I shall cry off altogether!"

"But you can't — he's asked Lord Pamyngton, too, and you know very well that Pam won't enjoy it unless you are there."

"Stuff!" Georgiana tossed her red-gold curls, which tonight were piled high on her head in Grecian style, and confined by a green and gold ribbon. "Pam won't complain while there are men enough in the house to make up a shooting party, or some other sporting expedition. It's altogether too much to ask me to endure the company of all the Curshawe family at once!"

"Hush, she will hear you," whispered Susan, with a warning glance at her neighbour."

"Much I care," retorted the irrepressible Georgy. "But if you're afraid of being overheard, let's move, Sue — I'm sure you would like a glass of lemonade, or something, and there will be no one in the refreshment room at present, so we can be as unguarded as we wish in what we say."

Susan obligingly rose, and with a quick word of excuse to the older ladies accompanied her sister-in-law across the crowded salon in the direction of the refreshment room.

"And to think George once fancied *you!*" went on Georgiana, in disgust. "It's beyond belief that he could turn to such a — mouse — as Caroline Curshawe after that!"

Susan coloured a little. "That was a long time ago, Georgy — and, anyway, you know very well it was only calf-love." She laughed. "Do you not recall how quickly he recovered from it when I made him drive me to my grandfather's house in Middlesex, and his favourite horse injured itself on the way?[1] I never saw such a change in anyone — I should

---

[1] See *The Clandestine Betrothal*

have found it most upsetting, had it not happened to be the very thing I was praying for!"

"Oh, yes!" Georgy laughed in her turn. "But a horse, Sue! You cannot expect to compete with such a powerful rival! You must know by now, even if you didn't realize it then, that the Eversley men think the world of their horses."

"All the same," said Susan, as they threaded their way among small groups of people who were chatting together, "I think Caroline's exactly the kind of girl he needs. She has an amiable, yielding disposition, and George likes to have his own way. Surely that promises well for their domestic happiness?"

Georgiana made a face. "Domestic happiness! Is that the recipe you and Hugh have for it? One to do all the giving, and the other all the taking? It wouldn't suit me, I promise you! Not unless I am to be the one who's doing the taking!"

By now they had reached the room where some light refreshments were set out. Georgiana guided Susan to a chair, and handed her a glass from the tray

8

which was quickly brought over to them by a watchful footman.

"We shall be out of earshot, here, at any rate," she went on, looking around. "For a while, that is to say. It will fill up presently — or someone will come in search of us."

Susan sipped her lemonade, considering her sister-in-law thoughtfully over the rim of the glass. She and Georgiana were old friends, for they had been at school together. She knew she could speak frankly.

"I'm worried about you, Georgy," she said, at last.

Georgiana arched her delicate eyebrows and smiled incredulously. "About me? Why?"

Susan frowned, her dark eyes troubled. "You seem so restless, my love. I can't help feeling that you would be a great deal happier if you were to marry."

Georgy gave a short laugh. "Oh, it's always the same with you wedded folk! You can't wait to hustle everyone else into your state of slavery. I'm very well as I am, I thank you. I am mistress of my father's home, and more or less free to do as I please. What possible advantages could marriage bestow on me? It's different for girls who are subject to tiresome parental rule — such females may very well wish to have an establishment of their own."

"But do you not find yourself longing for a companion to share your life, for children? Surely when you see my little Maria you must wish that you, too, had a child!"

Georgy laid a gentle hand on Susan's arm. "Your baby Maria is a darling, Sue, and I love her as dearly as even you could wish. But why should I be at the trouble of getting my own children, when evidently you mean to keep me well supplied with delightful nieces and nephews? Besides, I fear I should make but an indifferent Mama."

"You can't tell," said Susan, wisely, "you may fancy you are not the least little bit maternal, but when you hold your own baby in your arms, it's a different story, believe me! But never mind that, Georgy — that's to come later. Tell me truly, now; is there no gentleman of all the many who pay you attentions, whom you would care to wed?"

Georgiana shook her head decisively.

"Not even my Lord Pamyngton?" persisted Susan. "I've often watched you together, and it seemed to me that you had a certain — liking — for him."

"Oh, Pam!" Georgy's mouth curved in a smile. "He's prodigious fun — the more so because he's quite content to indulge in a little light flirtation without trying to push matters to a declaration. Come to think of it, I don't believe his interest in me is any more serious than mine in him. That's what makes his company more agreeable to me than that of almost anyone else."

"All the same, I think you're wrong. I believe him to be very taken with you. He's biding his time, mark my words."

"Stuff!" replied Georgy, lightly. "Every man who escorts me to a ball doesn't have to be in love with me, you know!"

"But most of them are," retorted Susan. "You've had at least five offers of marriage, to my knowledge."

"Six," amended Georgy, her green eyes dancing mischievously. "Seven, if you count Walter Shayne asking me twice."

"There! You see, you're quite the toast of the Town!" exclaimed Susan. "And much good it does you, you ungrateful creature — with all those suitors, you still cannot find one to your liking."

"Pooh, they're all the same," said Georgy scornfully. "Except Pam, that is. He's a little different from the rest. But don't think" — she rounded accusingly on Susan, in time to catch a complacent look on her sister-in-law's face — "that I mean to marry him, or indeed anyone! I'm quite content as I am."

"And why not? Any lady might be content with much less," drawled a lazy voice. "Shame on you, Miss Georgiana, for hiding yourself away like this! It's positively shabby, I declare! Mrs. Eversley, your husband is looking all over for you, with a very harassed expression on his face. I must put him out of his misery at once, poor fellow — but here he comes, I see."

Both ladies looked up. The speaker was a tall, elegant man in his middle twenties, wearing the full evening dress of dark coat, white waistcoat and knee breeches, and with his fair hair swept back in the fashionable Brutus crop. Georgy's face coloured a little as she looked into the twinkling eyes of Viscount Pamyngton. Could he possibly have failed to hear the rest of her speech? She and Susan had been too intent on their conversation to notice him at once.

If he had heard, he gave no sign. "I was hoping to persuade you to dance," he continued, extending his hand with the evident intention of assisting her to rise.

"May I hope for that pleasure? Or aren't you in the mood for dancing at present?"

"Why not?" Georgy shrugged white shoulders which were attractively displayed by her low-cut gown of gold silk and gauze: emerald eardrops quivered and flashed with the movement. She rose lazily, and placed her hand lightly on his arm. "Lead on, Pam."

Beau Eversley took the seat which his sister had just left, and drew his wife's small hand into his own firm clasp. "And how is my love?"

She dimpled at him. "Oh, splendid, Hugh — never better!" She stared thoughtfully after the retreating forms of Georgiana and Viscount Pamyngton. "What is to become of Georgy, dearest? Do you think she will wed my Lord Pamyngton, after all?"

"God only knows." Evidently the subject did not greatly interest him. "She likes him well enough, it seems."

"I wish she would decide on someone!" said Susan, with a small sigh. "She is for ever receiving offers, but no one seems to suit her. All of them have been eligible in every way — excepting old Sir Percival Codicote," she added, with a shudder, "and no one could like him! But so handsome and spirited as she is, and already one and twenty . . . Surely she must be capable of falling in love with someone?"

He laughed. "I see you are just like all the other females, after all — matchmakers, the lot of you! Oh, yes, I'm very sure that Georgy's capable of falling in love, right enough. The thing is, being such a contrary female, she's probably waiting until someone totally *in*eligible turns up!"

Susan was not the only member of

14

the family to speculate about Georgy's matrimonial future. Evelina Cunningham had just been boring her husband with the same theme, when she was interrupted by her brother George coming up to them.

"Do me a kindness, Eve, and help entertain a friend of mine," he said, hurriedly. "The thing is, he scarcely knows anyone here; and what with doing the gallant by Caro, I can't find much time to take him in tow, myself. Getting engaged plays the very devil with a fellow's private life — things will be easier when we're married, for she can't expect that I should dance attendance on her, then — a fine cake I should look, shouldn't I? Not the thing at all to have a husband hanging about his wife — no offence meant, Cunningham?"

Cunningham grunted, and Eve laughed. "Oh, George, you are impossible! Very well, where is this friend of yours?"

"He's over there, talking to Caro," replied George, with a gesture of his head.

Evelina looked towards Caroline Curshaw, and saw that her companion was a young man with a crop of dark brown, curling hair. He was wearing a deep blue coat which fitted rather too tightly over his broad shoulders, and his cravat was negligently tied, but nevertheless there was an air of assurance about him.

"What kind of man is he?" asked Cunningham. "He has the look of a sportsman."

"Oh, yes — bruising rider, boxing, cricket — anything in that line," replied George. "A devil to go, is old Jock — I knew him when I was up at Oxford. Hadn't seen him for years, and chanced across him the other day, in St. James's St., so naturally I asked him here tonight. But I fancy such affairs aren't much in his line. Come over, and I'll present him to you."

The young man, whose name neither Eve nor her husband quite managed to catch, was duly presented, and remained chatting to them for some time in a voice that held traces of a Scottish accent. Eventually he offered diffidently to lead Eve into the dance, and she accepted.

"You'll find me a shade rusty, ma'am," he apologized, as they took their places.

16

"It's some time since I attempted anything of the kind."

With all the charm of the accomplished hostess that she was, Evelina set his fears at rest. But as the dance progressed, she could see that he had little need to apologize. He moved with a natural grace that a practised performer might have envied. At one stage, they passed close to Georgiana, who was dancing with Pamyngton, and he turned his head to look at her for a moment.

"Who is that splendid female in the gold dress, ma'am?" he asked Eve, spontaneously. "She's the kind of girl who'll have no difficulty at all in producing a fine, healthy brood of children."

Evelina stared at him, too taken aback by this speech to make any immediate reply.

"I beg your pardon," he said quickly, noticing her surprise. "It's so long since I was in female company — I forget the observances of polite society."

"Pray do not regard it," replied Eve, recovering with an effort. "That is my younger sister, Georgiana. She is always very much admired." She added mentally that it was the first time she had ever heard Georgy admired in that particular manner.

He gave her a look of comical dismay. "Your sister? Oh, lord, ma'am, that makes it worse! What can I possibly say to redeem myself?"

Eve laughed. "There's no need to say anything. You couldn't know who she was — although you must have met her when you arrived?"

He grinned ruefully. "I fear I was late, ma'am, and the reception committee had dispersed. My own fault, but I was held up unavoidably."

They finished the dance next to Georgiana and her partner. Evelina sank into a curtsey, and the young man executed a graceful bow. As he bent forward, there was a sudden, loud rending sound. He clapped his hands between his shoulder blades, an almost comical look of dismay on his face.

"Oh, God!" he muttered, turning his head in an attempt to survey the damage. "I do believe I've split this damned coat, fiend seize it!"

There was a sudden splutter of laughter from Georgiana which she did very little to conceal. He turned a furious face towards her.

"It's not in the least funny, madam!"

Georgy laughed unrestrainedly at this. "I'm sorry, sir, but I can't help it! And, anyway, if you will be such a dandy as to wear a coat that's too tight for you — "

She continued to laugh; Evelina and Pamyngton were hard put to it not to follow her example.

"Allow me to inform you, madam," said the Scotsman, in biting tones, "that this coat is too tight only because I haven't worn it lately. I have neither the leisure nor the inclination to become a dandy."

"Nor the aptitude?" murmured Georgy, sweetly, her laughter subsiding a little in face of his anger.

He opened his mouth to retort, then closed it with a snap. He turned away from her, and addressed himself to Evelina.

"I'll escort you to your husband, ma'am," he said stiffly, "and then I'll

19

withdraw, with your permission."

With a reproachful look at her sister, Evelina accepted his arm. The young man bore her away carrying himself like a ramrod. Georgiana looked after them, then gave away to helpless laughter again, infecting her partner.

After a moment, he said, "Who is that fellow? Would you like me to teach him better manners?"

She shook her head, still laughing. "No, let be, Pam! My own manners were somewhat at fault, I fear, but I just couldn't help it — it was all so droll!" She sobered a little. "I've no notion who he can be, though he sounded as though he came from north of the Border, don't you think?"

"Can anything good come out of Scotland?" asked Pamyngton, with an indulgent smile. "Let's join the others, Miss Georgy, and forget all about the churlish fellow."

2

Reckless Young Woman

THE white road stretched invitingly ahead in the mellow October sunshine. The girl in the curricle felt a sudden urge for speed take hold of her, and gave the sign to her horses, a powerful pair of chestnuts. They leapt forward in an easy stride, their backs glowing in the sun like brown velvet. Her hold on the reins was light, but expert. Her green eyes glinted with ecstasy; the breeze blew back her fashionable bonnet, disclosing the richness of her auburn hair.

Her companion, a young woman of much the same age, attired in a loose yellow gown which could not conceal the fact that she was pregnant, clung convulsively to her seat.

"Georgy!" she pleaded, in a soft voice. "Pray do not go so fast!"

"Fast?" Georgiana Eversley laughed,

and tossed her auburn head in a reckless gesture that her sister-in-law recognized with misgiving. "You can't call this fast, Susan — why, they've scarce stretched their legs yet! Lud, they're prime steppers! I'll say this for Hugh — he's a prodigious judge of horseflesh!"

Susan Eversley swallowed hard, and made a brave attempt to conceal her dislike of the speed at which they were travelling. "I only hope he won't be vexed when he learns that we've taken them out," she said.

"Why should he?" retorted Georgiana, keeping her eyes on the road. "He said I could try them out some time. Now, didn't he?"

Susan agreed doubtfully. "All the same, I think he meant that you should drive them when he was beside you."

"Pooh! That would be poor sport, indeed, with Hugh telling me not to do this and that! I had far rather try out their paces on my own. Besides, what else are we to do, I'd like to know, with all the gentlemen of our party gone out shooting?"

"We could have joined the other ladies

on their walk," suggested Susan. "Or we could have played in the nursery with little Maria," she added, wistfully.

"Well, we'll play with baby Maria this afternoon," promised Georgy, in a milder tone. "But as for joining the others in walking down to the village to buy some more silks for that everlasting embroidery of theirs — pooh, I had far rather be dashing along in style like this, wouldn't you?"

"Ye-es," said Susan, doubtfully, staring at the road in rising trepidation. "But do slow up, Georgy — recollect there's a bend in the road just ahead, before we reach the gates."

Georgiana's laugh rang out clearly through the air. "What a piece of work you make, Sue!" she exclaimed. "Don't you trust me? You'll see, I'll take the curricle safely round the bend without any check in our speed! Do you care to wager on it? Your jade brooch against those diamond earrings of mine which you so much admire — is't a bargain?"

But Susan was too terrified to answer as the equipage swept round the bend in a whirl of dust.

Disaster was upon them before Georgy's undoubted skill and quick wits could do anything to avert it. Immediately before them was a gig drawn by a single horse. It had been approaching the bend in the road with caution and keeping well over to its own side; but the road was narrow at this point, and Georgy had swerved over to the wrong side in rounding the bend. The owner of the gig let out an angry shout, and pulled his placid mare up sharply. Georgy tugged desperately at the reins in a vain attempt to swerve away from the gig so that she could pass it in safety. The chestnut horses responded magnificently, avoiding a head-on collision; but they came abruptly to a halt, rearing, as the outside wheels of both vehicles locked together. The curricle stopped with a shuddering jerk that caused both ladies to fall forward on to the footboard. Luckily they were not thrown into the road.

The driver of the gig had lost his hat at the moment of collision. He ran his fingers through his crisp dark hair in a gesture of irritation, as he quickly leapt down to the ground.

"Hell and damnation!" he exclaimed, angrily. "Just what are you about, madam! D'ye wish to make an end of yourself? You may do it with my right goodwill, but have the charity to wait until only yourself is involved! Damme if I ever saw such cow-handed driving — you're not fit to have charge of a rocking horse!"

Without waiting for any reply, he signalled to a youth who had been sitting beside him in the gig.

"Here, Tom, you may safely leave Nelly. Try what you can do to help me quieten these two prime bits of blood, there's a good fellow."

The lad obediently vaulted from the gig to join his companion, who had seized the bridles of the two chestnuts in his short, strong hands, and was trying to calm the frightened beasts. Evidently the boy was good with horses; for after a moment the dark young man was able to leave him in charge, and come back to the occupants of the curricle.

He found they had picked themselves up and were crouching side by side on the seat, white-faced and subdued. Susan was trembling violently. He glanced at her sharply, then, jumping on to the step, snatched up a rug which was lying at her feet, and draped it round her.

He turned a furious face on Georgiana.

"B'God, my fine madam, if this lady loses her child, she'll know who to thank! Of all the downright criminal starts to get up to — "

Georgy's face turned from white to red. Like Susan, she had suffered a severe shock; moreover, she had twisted her ankle in some way when she had fallen, and it was beginning to pain her. She turned on her accuser, her eyes flashing green fire.

"Mind your manners, you — you clodpole, or it may be the worse for you!" she threatened. "Do you know who it is you're addressing? I am sister to Mr. Eversley at Fulmer Towers." She noticed with satisfaction that he gave a start at these words, and stared at her for a moment. "Yes, I thought that would change your tune! You are most likely some tenant who farms his land, I dare say. Well, you may find yourself out on your ear soon enough, if your tongue doesn't learn more discretion!"

His look changed to one of contempt. In spite of its hostile expression, she noticed that his face was almost handsome, with a strong mouth and a pair of deep, expressive brown eyes. She knew a momentary doubt. He had neither the air nor the accent of a local farmer. Moreover, she had a sudden conviction that she had seen him before somewhere, though the exact memory escaped her.

"You may be sister to the devil himself for all I care," he replied, in blighting tones. "Nay, I dare swear you are! Still, if you're from the Towers, as you say — "

"Do you presume to doubt my word!" stormed Georgy, at that moment far from being her usual rational self. Not only was she suffering from shock, but feelings of guilt were creeping over her. She ought to have thought of Susan, she knew, but somehow she had forgotten her sister-in-law's delicate condition in her own strong impulse to drive the chestnuts. And Susan was never one to fuss, which made it all the easier for others to overlook her claims to consideration. Georgy was beginning to feel furious with herself, and this insolent young man would do very well as a scapegoat. He even seemed set on filling the rôle.

"I might at that," he retorted, sarcastically. "But that doesn't signify at present. What does, is that this lady" — he bent over Susan and took one of her trembling hands in his, placing his fingers over her wrist — "should be conveyed home and to her bed instantly."

"How dare you take Mrs. Eversley's hand in that presumptuous way!" exclaimed Georgy, indignantly. "Let me inform you that when my brother comes to hear of it, he'll most likely take a horsewhip to you!"

"He'd do better to take it to you, madam," was the careless reply, as the young man released Susan's hand and jumped down from the step of the curricle. He turned an amused face upon Georgiana, who was now almost speechless with rage. "Don't be foolish — I'm a doctor, and would have been calling upon Mrs. Eversley in a professional capacity later on today, in any event."

He walked round to the locked wheels, and surveyed them frowningly, then addressed the boy Tom. "Let's see what can be done here."

It was Georgy's turn to stare. A doctor! He was not the doctor who usually attended her brother's family, she knew. That was a much older man called Hume. She turned to Susan, and put an arm about her.

"Sue, are you all right? I'm sorry — I never thought — I suppose I was too impulsive — and selfish — "

Susan nodded, making an effort to control the chattering of her teeth. "Yes — don't w-worry — I'm just c-cold — "

"Lud!" exclaimed Georgiana, as an unwelcome thought suddenly struck her. "Hugh will just about slaughter me for this! What with *you* and the horses — "

"We w-won't tell him, if you'd r-rather not — "

"Stuff! Why, this impudent fellow here will take the matter out of our hands, you may be sure! Sue, is he indeed your doctor? What's happened to the other man, Dr. Hume?"

"He's away at p-present. I w-was told

that his nephew w-would c-call during his absence," explained Susan, still shivering spasmodically.

"Here, you mustn't take cold," said Georgy, wrapping the rug more tightly about her sister-in-law.

Meanwhile the doctor and Tom had been carrying out manoeuvres which had eventually succeeded in unlocking the outside wheels of the two vehicles. The doctor looked dubiously at the wheel of the curricle, and then transferred his glance to Georgy's face.

"That wheel's almost wrenched off," he said. "You'd both best transfer to my vehicle, and let young Tom take the curricle back. But don't think I shall let you drive, ma'am — even poor old Nell, though Lord knows she's docile enough. I'll lead her. It's not far. Come Mrs. Eversley, you may safely trust yourself to me."

He walked round to Susan's side, and held out his arms to help her down to the road.

"Don't go, Sue!" cried Georgiana. "I have no intention of accepting this — *gentleman's*" — she accented the

30

word bitingly — "escort! We may quite well drive home by ourselves!"

"What, and land the curricle in the ditch before you've gone a yard?" He smiled sardonically, and, reaching up to Susan, gently assisted her to alight. "Come, ma'am," he continued, in a brisk, but reassuring tone. "You'll be comfortable enough in the gig for that short distance. And at least it's in no danger of heeling over at any minute, as your vehicle is."

Susan turned an imploring look on her sister-in-law.

"Pray c-come, Georgy!"

"I have no intention of leaving this seat!" Georgiana announced, heroically, setting her lips in a firm line.

"Then, p-perhaps," began Susan doubtfully, turning away from the doctor, "p-possibly I ought not — not t-to come — " She was stopped from finishing by a fit of shivering.

The doctor drew the rug more closely about her, and shook his head. "We'll settle that, ma'am, never you worry. Now, come along."

He helped her carefully into the gig,

then turned about purposefully.

"And now for you, Miss Eversley!" he said, a glint in his dark eyes.

Before Georgiana could guess what he intended, he had reached up and lifted her bodily from the curricle. She struggled for a moment as he bore her to the gig, but his arms were unexpectedly strong, and she was forced to submit. He dumped her beside Susan as if she had been a bundle of washing.

"You've hurt your foot," he said quickly, seeing her wince as her foot touched the floorboard. "Maybe a sprained ankle — I'll take a look when we get you home."

"You'll do no such thing," retorted Georgy; but for the moment some of the fire had gone out of her repartee.

He did not bother to answer, but picked up Nelly's reins and nodded to Tom. "You go on, lad, I'll need to turn, and this is a bad place for that. Don't put the wind up them at the Manor, now. Explain shortly that the two ladies are quite safe, and on their way home in another conveyance."

"Conveyance!" scoffed Georgy. She

said no more, however, sitting hunched up with an air of defeat, although inwardly she was seething. The only person who had ever dared to treat her in so high-handed a fashion was her brother, Hugh, whom she both adored and respected. To everyone else, and particularly to the male section of her acquaintance, she was the dashing Miss Eversley, who was above criticism, the Incomparable whose lightest whim must be obeyed.

She stared resentfully at the young man's back as he neatly turned the old mare and led her back along the road in the direction of Fulmer Towers. At any other time, she might have approved the firm set of his broad shoulders, and his swift, confident handling of the situation. As it was, she decided that it was easy to see from the way he carried himself that he was of a stubborn, autocratic disposition. Well, Hugh would soon give him the set-down he deserved, she reflected savagely. But where in the world had she seen this objectionable young man before? The recollection refused to come to her.

When the gig finally drew up before the doors of the house, a great commotion awaited them. Tom, who had managed to bring the curricle back without further damage, had followed his master's instructions to the letter; but he had not been able to allay all the alarm that had naturally been raised at his news. The ladies of the house party, now returned from their walk, crowded round the windows overlooking the drive. At first sight of the gig they flew to the door, and helped Susan indoors amid anxious twitterings and cluckings.

Georgiana found herself forgotten for the moment. She started to rise, but winced as she put her right foot to the floor. She hastily raised it again, transferring her weight to the other leg and clutching at the side of the gig for support.

"For all the world like a clutch of broody hens!" muttered the young man, looking after the ladies as they swept indoors with Susan in a flurry of petticoats. "They needn't worry — yon lass will take no lasting harm." He turned to Georgy, and, seeing her predicament, pushed her gently back into the seat. "What of you?" he asked, with a swift smile that was very disarming. "Let me take a look at that ankle."

"I'll do no such thing!" said Georgy, indignantly.

"Come, it's no time to be missish when you may have sustained an injury. It's my belief it's only trifling, but we'd best make sure."

Georgy flung him a withering look, and tugged at the hem of her green wool riding dress, so that it completely covered her ankles. His smile broadened into an attractive grin.

"I'll wager you're not always so modest," he told her.

The look in Georgiana's eyes would have totally routed any of the gentlemen of her own circle. Her face flamed, but her voice was ice-cold as she asked, "What is your name, fellow?"

He sketched a mocking bow. "John Graham, at your service, ma'am. Doctor of Medicine, and a surgeon at St. George's Hospital, in London."

"Then, Dr. Graham," she replied, speaking very slowly and distinctly, "kindly go about your own business, whatever that may be. You will, of course, require your — *conveyance* — before you can do so. Will you have the goodness — I should not ask it of you, but unfortunately there seems to be no one else in the vicinity at present — to call one of the servants to help me indoors?"

He threw back his head and laughed delightedly. "You're a rare one!" he exclaimed. "There's nothing wrong with you that a good spanking wouldn't put right, after all! And if your brother Hugh's anything like your brother George, you'll most likely get one, too, for damaging his curricle."

Georgy was almost betrayed into civility by surprise. "Do you know George?"

"Lord, yes! We were at Oxford together, though he wasn't in my year — I'm his senior. Couldn't help running across him, though — everyone knew George Eversley. Of all the — " He broke off. Georgy's face, which had begun to show some interest in the conversation, froze over again.

"No doubt," she said, tartly, "you were about to make one of your odiously impertinent remarks — this time about my brother George. I don't wish to have anything more to say to you, Dr. Graham. Kindly send someone to my assistance."

"Who better than myself?" he asked, swooping down suddenly and gathering her up into his arms.

"Put me down instantly — instantly!" stormed Georgy, losing her cold disdain all at once, and beating a tattoo on his chest with her fists. "How dare you!"

"You should never dare a Scot," he warned her, laughing. "And if I were to obey you, and put you down instantly, you would be suffering from more than a twisted ankle when you made contact with this gravel. Shall I try it?"

He dropped his arms a few inches as though he meant to dump her on the drive. She let out a stifled scream, and clung to him.

"Oh! You are intolerable — the greatest beast in nature — I detest you, and hope I may never set eyes on you again!"

"You're a termagant," he countered, with a twinkle in his eye, as he mounted the steps to the house. "But you're a

37

very agreeable armful, all the same. As for not seeing me again, there's no hope of that while you remain here in Buckinghamshire with your brother. I am acting here as locum for my uncle, Dr. Hume, who has been obliged to go up to Scotland for a few weeks on family affairs. And as Dr. Hume is physician to your brother's family when they are down here in the country, I shall be frequently calling in to see how Mrs. Eversley goes on."

"I can say no more!" exclaimed Georgy, in outraged tones. "Your manners disgust me — your ill-bred familiarity! But one can expect nothing else, I suppose, from one of your profession! A *surgeon*" — she pronounced the word with loathing — "a low creature who does the most unspeakable things!" She shuddered theatrically.

He nodded. "Indeed, yes," he agreed, dryly. "Unspeakable things that now and then may manage to save a man's life."

The house door was ajar. He shouldered his way in with Georgiana in his arms just as a footman, belatedly recollecting his duty, appeared in the hall, and opened the door of the nearest room. Dr. Graham was able to deposit his lovely burden, whose beauty was at present marred by the vengeful expression on her face, upon a sofa. Before she could prevent him, he had taken her right ankle between his short, strong fingers, and gently examined it.

He nodded, satisfied. "You've only twisted it," he said, "just as I thought. Cold water bandages, and you'll need to keep off it for the rest of the day. Should be as right as a trivet by tomorrow. All the same, I'll give you a look-in tomorrow forenoon, when I'll be waiting upon Mrs. Eversley."

"Thank you," replied Georgiana, with cold dignity, "but I shall not be requiring your services."

He chuckled. "Who shall say? Especially when your brother has done with you — though it may not be your ankle that is paining you then! Well, I must look to my real patient. I dare say they'll have got her into bed by now. To our next meeting, Miss Eversley, ma'am!"

He sketched a bow and went swiftly out of the room.

She screwed up her face in an expression of rage, and stamped her good foot.

"Hell and damnation!" exclaimed the unladylike Miss Eversley.

Fortunately, she was quite alone.

3

The Doctor Pays A Visit

SUSAN was soon restored by a short rest, but Georgiana suffered more lasting effects from the recent mishap. Her ankle was painful for the rest of the day, and she was forced to follow the advice she would have preferred to spurn, and to sit about with her leg raised on a footstool. Inactivity was always irksome to her, and it did nothing to soothe her feelings of rancour towards the young doctor who had treated her in so high-handed a fashion. Besides, her thoughts made unpleasant company. As the day wore on towards the time when the gentlemen could be expected back from their day's sport, she became more than a little apprehensive.

She was not the only one. Susan had misgivings which she was careful to keep to herself; and Aunt Lavinia, who was to remain with the Eversleys until after the birth of their second child, did not scruple to voice hers.

"If Hugh gives you a good dressing down, miss, it will be no more than you deserve!" she declared, with all the freedom of a relative who had held Georgy as a baby on her knee. "I should have known better, I suppose, than to leave the pair of you alone! I might have guessed you'd be up to some mischief the moment my back was turned. It was always the same!"

"In that case, I'm glad I didn't disappoint you, Aunt," replied Georgy, tartly.

Aunt Lavinia bridled. "I want none of your impudence, miss! When I was a girl of your age, I would never have dared to speak so to my aunt — "

"I am one-and-twenty," returned Georgy, wearily. "You talk as if I were still a schoolgirl."

"Then you shouldn't behave like one. At your age, you should have outgrown all such hoydenish pranks, and acquired the conduct befitting a young lady of rank. Your father had best hurry up and find you a husband — marriage should give a more proper direction to your thoughts, though sometimes I doubt even that!"

"Aren't you perhaps being a little severe on her, ma'am?" asked Margaret Radley, another of the visitors. She was the wife of one of Beau Eversley's closest friends, and by nature a peacemaker. "She really does drive very well, you know, in general. I know of no other female who could possibly handle the kind of horses Hugh keeps in his stable. She was just unfortunate — or perhaps it was this young doctor's fault, after all."

"Good of you, Margaret," said Georgy, brusquely. "But it won't do, I fear. I was well over on my wrong side, as it happens."

Miss Caroline Curshawe said shyly that perhaps there might have been a little — a very little — error of judgment on both sides. Her mother, Mrs. Curshawe, who was the remaining lady of the party, pursed her lips and was silent. Privately, she considered that Georgiana's conduct too often exceeded the bounds of propriety. Of course, since Lady Eversley's death three years ago, the girl had been more or less her own mistress. She lived at home with her father, who indulged her in every possible way, even to the lengths of allowing her to dispense with the services of an older female to act as chaperon. No doubt he considered a resident chaperon unnecessary when Georgiana could always call on either her elder sister or her sister-in-law to act in that capacity. But as both Evelina Cunningham and Susan Eversley were mothers of young families, it was hardly to be expected that they would devote much of their time to Georgiana's concerns. What was certain, thought Mrs. Curshawe scornfully, was that these ladies seemed to have not the slightest influence on their wayward young relative. She did as she pleased, and always seemed to be an object of admiration to those surrounding her.

The Curshawes had naturally been delighted when George Eversley had offered for their youngest daughter: it was a splendid match. But since accepting Hugh Eversley's invitation for Caroline, herself and her son Henry to join a party at his house in the

44

country for a few weeks, Mrs. Curshawe had constantly been assailed by doubts. The fashionable Eversleys were reputed to have a wild streak, and Georgiana's conduct daily bore witness to the truth of this. She began to recall some of the rumours concerning her host that had run round the Town at one time. It was scarcely fair to bring these up again now, for he was certainly a changed man since marrying that obscure little Miss Susan Fyfield. Still, the streak was there in the family. She fervently hoped for Caroline's sake that by now George Eversley at least might have finished sowing his wild oats; and that his unruly sister might not involve them all in some dreadful scandal before she, too, learnt sense, and settled down to a way of life more becoming to a gently-reared female. After all, it was one thing for gentlemen to be a bit wild. In a way, it was almost expected of them. It was quite another, thought Mrs. Curshawe disapprovingly, for a young lady to be so heedless of convention.

Georgiana was paying no attention to her companions. Her ankle was causing her a certain amount of discomfort, but her thoughts were a more serious cause of unease. Although she generally followed her own inclination, paying little heed to the criticism of others, she was not immune from self-criticism. This would often be the more searching of the two, for hers was a frank, honest nature. Any mistaken notions she entertained were never the result of deliberate self-deception. Now she freely acknowledged that she ought not have taken Susan out with her in Hugh's curricle. The truth of the matter was that she always found it difficult to think of Susan in any other way than as the schoolgirl with whom she had shared so many escapades in the past. She had overlooked the fact that her friend was now a wife and soon to give birth to a second child. She told herself that she had been thoughtless, and might have caused serious harm to Susan, as that detestable Dr. Graham had not scrupled to remind her.

It was enough for her to accuse herself: but what in the world was Hugh going to say? As the time drew near when he might be expected home, her trepidation mounted. If only he would come quickly, so that she could get it over and done with! She had never been one to postpone an unpleasant ordeal that must eventually be faced.

At length, sounds were heard of the returning party. Her heart began to beat unpleasantly fast, and, but for the wretched ankle, she would have taken herself off to her bedroom until she felt calm enough to face Hugh. Clearly this was impossible, so she steeled herself for the ordeal, her face achieving an interesting pallor as the moments of suspense ticked away.

They all entered the room together, laughing and chatting, and Hugh paid no heed to Georgy, but went at once to his wife's side. She heaved a little sigh of relief for the respite, but it was short-lived. Both Pamyngton and Henry Curshawe had no eyes for anyone but herself after a day's absence. They came towards her, and at once demanded to be told why she was resting one leg upon a footstool.

"Oh, it's nothing," she answered, airily. "I've twisted my ankle a bit, that's all.

It will be perfectly well tomorrow, I dare say. Did you have a good day's sport?"

Pamyngton was a perceptive man, and saw at once that she wanted no fuss. But Curshawe, whose ardour for Georgy had been increased since coming to the Towers by the presence of a formidable rival, was determined not to be backward in any attentions. He plied her with questions about the injury in such an earnest tone that he drew Hugh's notice to her.

"What's this? Hurt yourself, Georgy? How?"

Susan made frantic signals with her eyes to stop her sister-in-law from replying. "Poor Georgy!" she said hurriedly. "And it was all my fault, Hugh! I fear you're going to be very vexed with me!"

He smiled at her, and raised a quizzical eyebrow.

"Vexed with you, my love? Vastly, I dare swear! Very well, you'd better confess — what have you been up to this time? Though I'll wager," he added, "that it's six of one and half a dozen of the other, if Georgiana's concerned in the business."

Georgy started to speak, but Susan frowned her down. "You — will be vexed, I know," she said, turning a timid look on her husband. "You see, we — I, that is — wanted to go for a drive. And so we took out your curricle, with the chestnut pair — "

"You did *what*?" Beau Eversley stared at his wife.

"I know it was foolish — and wrong — "

"That's not it, Hugh," put in Georgy, quietly. Now that the moment of revelation had come, she was quite calm. She raised her tawny head in a proud gesture as she felt Hugh's outraged gaze upon her. "You're very good, Sue, but don't think I mean you to take the blame. It was my idea, Hugh, and I persuaded Sue to come with me."

He nodded. "Yes, that certainly sounds more likely. Do you mind telling me" — his lazy drawl did not deceive either of them for a moment into mistaking his feelings — "exactly what befell my horses, since you didn't manage to escape injury?"

"Oh, they're quite safe, Hugh!" put in Susan, quickly. "There was just — well — there is only the wheel of the curricle which is not quite — not quite — "

"Not quite as good as it was, I think you would say, my love?" The Beau's tone was mild.

"I assure you, Hugh, the horses are sound in wind and limb," said Georgy. "I sent round to the stables for a report, as soon as Susan was settled — "

"Susan," interrupted Hugh, gently, turning a reflective eye on his wife. "Yes, to be sure, Susan. I think perhaps, Georgiana, you and I will discuss that aspect of the affair later, in private."

Georgy nodded, but her heart sank. She could foresee a most unpleasant interview. Hugh was not one to fume and storm, but he had a quiet technique of his own which could bring home an offence far more effectively.

"What exactly happened?" asked Freddy Eversley. "Did the chestnuts bolt with you?"

"No such thing!" answered Georgy,

her pride stung. "I came round the bend — the one just before the gates, you know — a trifle fast, and there was this stupid gig, driven by the most odious man, with positively execrable manners — "

Freddy grinned. "Can't blame the chap if he was rude, when you obviously muffed the whole thing," he said, with a brother's brutal frankness.

"You're the greatest beast in nature!" retorted Georgy, equally frank. "I did *not* muff it, did I, Sue?" Fortunately, she did not pause for her sister-in-law to answer, but continued, "And anyway, if you could have heard the way he spoke to me — *and* treated me — I feel sure any of you, Hugh, George or even you, Freddy, would have called him to account. Although, of course," she added, reflectively, "I'm not sure that you could, as he's not precisely a gentleman — "

"Had a dust-up with a tradesman, did you?" asked George, turning from his betrothed for a moment. "Well, I dare say you deserved anything he may have said to you. You ought to know by now that you can't career round that bend, Georgy; the road's too narrow there. Damn it all, you're a fair whip — for a female," he added cautiously.

"Thank you very much! But he wasn't exactly a tradesman — he was a doctor, and what's more, he said he knew you at Oxford."

"So did a good many people," replied George. "What was his name?"

"John Graham," replied Georgy, with her nose elevated.

"John Graham — old Jock? Is he down here?" asked George, with increased interest. "He's a rattling good chap — you must have met him at our evening party in Town last month, Georgy, for he was there."

Georgy shook her head. "No, I'm sure I didn't. I don't recollect the name, although — " she paused, frowning. "Although I'm bound to say that I did have the impression I'd seen him before, somewhere — "

She broke off, then suddenly snapped her fingers in what Mrs. Curshawe privately considered an unladylike gesture.

"I recollect now!" she exclaimed, with

a laugh. "He was the young man who split his coat!"

"Oh, *that* man!" said Pamyngton, smiling. "It's no wonder he seized his chance to be revenged on you today, Miss Georgy. You certainly made him angry enough at the ball."

No one else in the room had any notion what they were talking about, as Dr. John Graham had evidently left the party without ceremony that evening after his unfortunate mishap. Georgy and Pamyngton proceeded to tell them the story in a lively duologue that did much to restore Georgy's spirits. When they had finished, there was a general laugh.

"Oh, ay, that sounds very like old Jock!" chuckled George. "He's always been one to speak his mind without fear or favour."

"It's an attribute that surely can do little to recommend him to his patients?" asked Mrs. Curshawe, in surprise.

"Perhaps not, ma'am. But I can tell you this — if I had anything seriously amiss with me, I'd as lief have old Jock to doctor me as any medico you'd care to name," replied George, defensively.

"I've watched him remove a bullet from a man's arm, as neat as shelling peas, and all over in a matter of minutes."

Several of the ladies shuddered.

"Pray, nephew, remember where you are!" said Aunt Lavinia, with a snap. "This is not a fit conversation for a drawing-room!"

"Oh, very well, Aunt, though I can't see what harm there is — " He met Hugh's eye, and coughed slightly. "I beg your pardon, Aunt Lavinia. All I meant to say is that Jock's a clever chap. But I wonder how he comes to be in this part of the country at all? He's a surgeon at St. George's Hospital, and his home's in Edinburgh, if I remember aright."

"I believe I can enlighten you on that point," said Hugh. "Dr. Hume waited upon me one day last week to let me know that he would be away in Scotland for the next few weeks, and that his nephew would be acting as locum until his return. He was anxious to assure me," he added, smiling at Susan, "that he would be back in good time for a certain important event in our family."

George nodded. "So Jock's your Dr.

Hume's nephew? Ay, I recollect now that he once told me he could trace his descent from the Earls of Home, a set of Border chieftains, seemingly, whom the Scots think a deal of. He said it was the same family — Home or Hume, however one likes to spell it — and I can remember him saying that he was kin to the surgeon John Hunter's wife, who was also of the same name."

"Oh, if you are talking of Mrs. Anne Hunter," broke in Aunt Lavinia, "I know of her. Harry Walpole used to attend her soirées at one time, poor man; though of course he is dead now. One still feels his loss! Not that I have any patience with that Bluestocking kind of female," she continued. "It's enough for a lady to look pretty and charming — men cannot abide a clever woman."

"No, indeed," agreed Georgy, ironically. "She presents too much of a challenge to male superiority, does she not?"

"I must say that comes well from a cow-handed female who comes a cropper the first time she takes out a pair of blood horses!" remarked Freddy, provocatively.

Georgy coloured up, and bit back

an angry retort. Hugh raised his brows comically, and Aunt Lavinia called her nephew sharply to order for his use of a vulgar expression only fit to be employed in male society.

"If you think so, Aunt, then you'd best reprove Dr. Graham when he calls," said Georgy, still looking annoyed. "He used the exact phrase to describe my driving."

There was an outburst of laughter from her brothers at this. Pamyngton bit his lip hard in an effort not to follow their example, but Curshawe frowned.

"If this man has said or done anything to distress you, ma'am, you have friends who would be only too willing to point out the error of his ways to him," he said, with heavy gallantry.

Georgiana turned to him with a swift smile of such charm that his heart gave a sudden leap.

"Thank you, Mr. Curshawe, you are very good. But I fancy I can deal with Dr. Graham myself."

"Revenge!" declaimed Freddy, striking an attitude. "What will you do, Georgy? We are all agog!"

"Never you mind," replied his sister, darkly.

"Tell you what," suggested the irrepressible Freddy, "you could always pay him out by taking him for a drive in Hugh's curricle."

"Very amusing!" retorted Georgy, icily. "To be sure, you are a great wit!"

"Come, you have teased your sister enough," said Hugh. "It's time we changed the subject, before our guests tire of it. Be good enough to ring the bell, Freddy, and we'll take a glass of sherry wine."

Before Freddy could comply with this request, there was a tap on the door, and a footman entered.

"Dr. Graham has called, sir."

4

The Wager

NORMALLY, Beau Eversley would have instructed the servant to show Dr. Graham into another room; but now some mischievous impulse prompted him to bring the doctor in amongst the assembled company. He was curious to see what Georgiana's reactions would be, and also to make the acquaintance of any man under the age of sixty who could remain impervious to the charms of the irresistible Miss Eversley.

From the first, he liked the look of John Graham. The young doctor was not of his own fashionable world, of course. Doctors rarely were, although there had been a few, such as Dr. William Hunter, who had succeeded in breaking into fashionable circles. This young man had the appearance of a country squire, with his brown coat, leather knee breeches and rather dusty boots. He was of a good height, though not quite as tall as either Beau Eversley himself or Viscount Pamyngton, but in the matter of shoulders he had a trifle the advantage of either. It was a good-humoured face, thought Beau Eversley; strong, yet capable of compassion, and with an air of integrity that inspired confidence. On the whole, he could understand George's faith in this man as a medico.

George Eversley at once came forward with outstretched hand, and greeted his friend heartily. After this, he presented him to the rest of the company. Dr. Graham acknowledged the introductions with a quick, curt bow, and a smile that twisted one side of his mouth in an attractive way.

"I think you've already met my sister Georgiana," said George, with a twinkle in his eye.

Graham bowed. "I've had that honour." Georgiana flashed a suspicious look at him, but his voice was non-committal. "Indeed, I came to inquire for the health of the two ladies, after their — "

he paused momentarily — "unfortunate mishap this forenoon."

"Good of you, my dear chap, but they're little the worse, though Georgy has ricked her ankle a trifle. Still, if she will make such a cake of herself — "

Georgy flashed an indignant look at her brother.

"It's a tricky bend just there," said Graham, diplomatically.

If he had hoped to placate her, he only made matters worse, as both he and George plainly saw from her face.

"How is the ankle, ma'am?" he went on. "I see you are taking my advice, and resting it."

Evidently this did not please her, either. "Was that your advice?" she queried, coldly. "I'm afraid I did not attend. I found for myself that it was easier this way."

"You very well might, ma'am," he said, gravely, though his mouth twitched. "It isn't the most closely guarded of medical secrets, after all."

She gave him a look of disdain, then turned her back on him and summoned Pamyngton over to her chair.

He came willingly, followed inevitably by Curshawe, who was determined that the Viscount should not steal a march on himself in Miss Georgy's good graces.

"Are you here for long, Jock?" asked George, leading his friend over to the knot of men who had gathered about the tray of drinks which had just been brought into the room.

"Three or four weeks at most," replied Graham. "My uncle will conclude his business as soon as he can. He's anxious to return in plenty of time for Mrs. Eversley's confinement."

"Well, since you're so near to us, we must try and see something of you. Would you care to take a gun out in our company, now and then? And of course you'll be joining the Hunt."

"Thank you, I'd like to join you for a day's shooting, if my duties permit. But I fear hunting's out of the question — my uncle has no suitable horse in his stable, which consists solely of the old mare who pulls the gig. As for the horses the village innkeeper keeps for hire — well, perhaps you know their quality."

George laughed. "I do indeed. But

don't let that worry you — Hugh will mount you, won't you, Hugh?" He looked interrogatively at his elder brother. "I dare say we can find Jock something a bit better in the way of horseflesh than old Reddings at the Feathers keeps in his stable, eh? And you may take my word for it that old Jock's a first-rate rider — and a whip, too, come to that."

Hugh readily assented. Graham thanked him, but privately made up his mind not to take advantage of the offer. His Scots pride did not relish favours. He finished his glass, and spoke of going, but George demurred.

"Why don't you stay and dine with us?" he asked, hospitably. "Dinner will be on the table before long, and we'd be glad of your company."

Graham looked down at his dress. "I'm scarcely rigged for dining out," he protested.

"Oh, I dare say Susan will excuse you. We don't stand on ceremony in the country, you know. What do you say, Sue? Here's Jock refusing to stay and dine with us on account of his dress. Tell him it don't signify."

Susan did her part very prettily; but Graham was too perceptive not to see the veiled doubt on the faces of Mrs. Curshawe and Aunt Lavinia, and the open disgust on Georgiana's. It was enough for him.

"Thank you, ma'am, but I believe I must decline. I am expected back to dinner, and I wouldn't like to put my aunt to any inconvenience. Moreover" — quickly anticipating an offer to send a message by a servant — "there are one or two matters awaiting my attention in the surgery. We have no apothecary here in the village, you know, and my uncle is in the way of doing a fair bit of his own dispensing."

After a few protests, which were politely but firmly overborne, the doctor had his way. George then proposed that he should dine with them on the following day, and as the invitation was charmingly echoed by Susan, it would have been churlish to give a second refusal. The engagement was fixed, and the doctor took his leave.

"In my day," remarked Aunt Lavinia,

when he had gone, "no one would have dreamt of asking the leech to dine. I should have liked to have seen Papa's face if any of us had suggested such a thing!"

"Very likely," agreed Beau Eversley, smoothly. "But times change, my dear aunt, and we are starting on a new century, after all. Besides, it is not the doctor whom we have invited to dine, but a friend of George's."

"Yes, and if you want to be so confounded uppity, Aunt," put in George, "I'll have you know that old Jock's a gentleman, right enough. Besides being a descendant of these confounded Border chieftains of his, he's also kin to some deuced Scottish laird, with an unpronounceable name, and in direct line for the title, whatever it is. Damn it, the chap was at Oxford with me, as Hugh says, anyway. That should be enough."

Fortunately, dinner was announced at this point, and the conversation turned on to ways of conveying Georgy to the dining-room, which was quite a distance away from the parlour where they were sitting, although it was on the same level. Pamyngton and Curshawe had their own reasons for favouring a chair lift which they were determined to operate themselves. Freddy settled the matter by sending for the chair on wheels which had been provided for Susan in case she should not feel like walking later on in her pregnancy.

Pamyngton and Curshawe were plainly set on helping her into the chair, but Georgy insisted on her two younger brothers performing that service for her. She felt just a little bored by her admirers' constant attentions. No sooner was she safely installed in the chair than Freddy seized the handle before anyone else could reach it, and began to propel the chair through the parlour door and along the passage at an alarming rate.

"Oh, pray be careful!" begged Georgy, clinging on to the sides of the chair. "I'll have a broken leg at this rate, you monster!"

He looked back over his shoulder for a second, then turned again quickly, ignoring the signals from the others whom they had now left behind.

"I don't mean to surrender you to

either of 'em!" he chuckled, in her ear. "Lord, did you ever see such a doting pair? Fair makes you v — " he changed the word quickly — "sick, don't it? Wonder what there can be about you, Georgy, that sends all the men wild for you? I can't see it, myself — you're not a bad-looking female, of course, as they go. But you're as mad as a hatter, and have a devil of a temper, besides."

"Thank you," replied his sister, icily. "Freddy, just you wait until you've injured a limb! I shall be sure to treat you to a ride in this chair, you may depend on't!"

"You'd most likely have the thing over, though, whereas I" — he swerved, narrowly avoiding an occasional table — "am in complete control, as you see."

Georgy suppressed a scream, and clung to the chair even more tightly. "If you say so."

"Y'know," went on Freddy, slowing down to steer her through the doors of the dining-room, "I dare say poor old Susan felt like you do now, when she was out with you this morning."

66

She turned her face up to him, and he was taken aback to see that her lip was quivering.

"It's ungenerous of you to say that. Don't think it hasn't occurred to me — "

He leaned over and patted her hand. "Sorry; you're not the only lunatic in the family. Anyway you'll feel better when Hugh's given you a drubbing. I never knew that fail to relieve any feelings of guilt one might be suffering from."

She did not answer, and he stood still for a moment, trying to think of a way to blot out the impression made by his tactless remarks. Like his sister, he had a kind and generous nature; but both of them sometimes allowed their tongues to outrun their discretion. Presently, he thought he had hit upon a way to drive his tactless words from her mind.

"I say, Georgy," he began, in a different tone, "I must say it made a welcome change to see the doctor don't dote on you, at any rate. Don't know when I ever came across anyone who was quite so indifferent to your charms — why, you might have been old Aunt Lavvy, for all the notice he took."

"I haven't the faintest desire to be noticed by such a man," replied Georgiana, loftily. "His admiration could only be an insult to any female of taste."

"Oh, I don't know," said her brother, reflectively. "He's not a bad-looking chap. I dare say he could be almost as much of a hit as Hugh was, if he'd a mind to — he's not one of your elegant Beaux, of course, more the sportsman — but there's definitely something."

"Well, whatever it is, I want none of it!"

He set the chair against a wall, and stood facing her, awaiting the rest of the party. There was a challenging smile on his face, and the Eversley devilment in his eyes.

"Are you sure, Georgy? Or aren't you just the slightest shade annoyed that Dr. Graham commits the heresy of remaining impervious to your charms?"

"No such thing!" retaliated his sister. "It's no matter to me! Believe me, if I had the smallest inclination to bring the obnoxious man to my feet — which I have *not* — I don't doubt my ability to accomplish it! So there!"

"I'll wager you couldn't," stated Freddy, emphatically.

"I've just told you I haven't the slightest wish — "

Her brother laughed. "Oh, ay, that's an easy way out! Sour grapes, eh?"

Georgiana tilted her chin in a dignified silence.

"Tell you what, though, Georgy," went on Freddy, as through the open door he watched the others approaching the room. "You were talking earlier on of getting your revenge on Graham. Wouldn't that be a capital way, if only you could do it? Which, of course, you can't, as I'm convinced — in fact, prepared to bet on it."

He looked down at his sister, and saw that her green eyes had suddenly started to glow.

"Are you, Freddy? Very well, then, why not? As you say, it would be a fitting revenge for his insolence — and, anyway, it will lend a little zest to a quiet stay in the country. What will you wager?"

He laughed, catching something of her

excitement; then he named a sum. She nodded.

"You won't have very long," he warned her. "And it must be accomplished while you're here in Buckinghamshire — that's part of the bargain."

"Done!" she agreed, recklessly.

"Well, I wish you luck, sister! But I'm bound to tell you that I believe I shall win."

"What will you win?" asked Pamyngton, who was first in the room.

"Oh nothing," replied Freddy airly. "Just a little private wager between Georgy and myself."

"I wonder Miss Georgiana is sufficiently in charity with you to enter into any friendly contract," remarked Curshawe, "after the way you tooled that chair along! I wished afterwards that one of us had taken it."

"Don't you worry about my sister," advised Freddy, with a surreptitious wink in Georgiana's direction. "She's a devil to go, aren't you, Georgy?"

5

Anne Hume Mends A Coat

WHEN John Graham returned home, he found his cousin Anne in the small room where her father kept the medicine, busy making up some potions from prescriptions which he had written out after he had done the morning's rounds. She looked up as he entered, and gave him a shy smile.

"It's good of you, Anne, but you shouldn't put yourself to this trouble," he said, shaking his head. "I'm sure you have enough calls on your time, as it is."

"I always do this for Papa," she explained, her small capable hands busy with the pestle and mortar. "I like the work. Besides, there is no sewing that Mama wants me to do at present, and I can't sit and do nothing."

"No, indeed. I've been here long enough to see that you are certainly no drone," he agreed, smiling at her, as he removed his coat, and rolled up his shirt sleeves. "And you're such a little thing, too, which makes your energy somewhat unexpected. No doubt about it, you're a fine, healthy girl, Anne."

She coloured up a little at this. "I wish you wouldn't, cousin John," she protested, gently.

"Wouldn't what?" He was genuinely puzzled.

"Wouldn't speak of people as though you saw only their physical attributes, and nothing of their minds or — or characters."

"Do I do that?" He paused in the act of reaching for a bottle from the medicine chest, reflecting for a moment. "Yes, perhaps I do. Well, I'm more concerned with bodies than minds in most of my work — though mark you, cousin, I believe that the mind has a powerful effect on the body at times." He broke off, frowning. "Perhaps I should devote some time to the study of that particular subject. That female I saw today, for instance. Of course, she's a fine, healthy specimen of womanhood," he continued, talking more to himself than to his cousin. "But I wonder what effect a mind and character such as hers — proud, bold, imperious — might have on the course of an illness, say — "

"What female?" asked Anne, keeping her head down over her work.

"The one who's staying at Fulmer Towers. Viscount Eversley's daughter, Georgiana. I dare say you'll have seen her hereabouts at some time?"

Anne shook her head, but still did not look up.

"She's magnificent," he said thoughtfully. "Firm, strong bones, and a good straight spine — no backboard was needed there, I'll be bound! One of those fine, creamy skins and a mass of softly curling auburn hair — a veritable Juno of a girl; only six inches or so shorter than I am."

"There you go again," accused Anne, still avoiding his eye. "What is she like, herself? Her character, I mean?"

"Oh, odious, I should imagine!" he answered, with a shrug. "Spoilt, arrogant, selfish — "

She smiled up at him, satisfied. "Did you meet her when you called on Mr. Eversley's wife?" she asked.

"Not exactly. Oh, Lord, that reminds me of something!" he concluded, in dismay.

She stopped work, raising her brows in a silent question.

"You said there was no sewing, Anne. I wonder, could you possibly repair something for me? I wouldn't ask, only there is no time now to buy another."

"You talk in mysteries, cousin John. What is there no time to buy? But certainly I will mend anything for you that you like."

"A coat — an evening dress coat. I split it last time I wore it. It's too small for me, really, but I haven't another, and there's no chance of borrowing one from anyone here, and no time to get to London to buy a new one."

"Papa has his coats made by a tailor in Amersham."

"Perhaps so; but if your man in Amersham can make me a coat by tomorrow evening, then he has all

74

the London tailors knocked into a cocked hat."

"Tomorrow evening?" echoed Anne.

He nodded. "Yes. I'm engaged to dine with the Eversleys."

"Oh!" She seemed surprised. "They have never asked Papa to dine," she finished, slowly.

"No, well, I knew George Eversley at Oxford," he explained, a little embarrassed by her tone. "They've offered to find me a mount for the hunt, too, which is good of them, don't you think? Not that I intend to take them up on it."

Whatever Anne thought, she was wise enough to keep to herself. After dinner was over, she asked him to fetch the coat; and, sitting in the parlour beside her mother, she began a neat, almost invisible repair of the torn seams.

She was still working on it when at last he came into the parlour, having finished putting up the medicines and despatched the boy Tom with the more urgent of them. He relaxed in a wing chair with a sigh of comfort.

"I'll have the tea brought in," said Mrs. Hume, rising to pull the bell over the old-fashioned chimney piece. "I dare say you can do with it, John. You've had a hard day of it."

"Oh, no, not too bad," he replied, running his fingers through his crisp, dark hair. "They work me harder than this at St. George's, Aunt Margery. But then most cases there are pretty desperate; while what have I had here, today? Two feverish chills, a broken arm, a gouty leg, a few putrid sore throats and one delivery. Oh, and I nearly forgot" — he laughed — "a twisted ankle."

"Surely no one would bother to call you in for that?" asked Mrs. Hume, indignantly.

"But it might be a broken bone, Mama," Anne reminded her. "It's always best to have an expert opinion."

"No one did call me in," put in Graham, "because I happened to be on the spot. I forgot to tell you I had a slight collision this morning. Oh, nothing serious" — as they both exclaimed in dismay — "our vehicle came off with scarce a scratch. Miss Eversley wasn't so fortunate — the wheel was almost wrenched off hers, and in addition she hurt her ankle. Nothing to speak of, though."

"I've heard she is rather wild, Miss Georgiana," remarked Mrs. Hume. "She quite often comes down to stay with her eldest brother, when the family is at the house here. I've seen her once or twice, riding or walking through the village — she's a very handsome young lady."

"I've never seen her," said Anne.

"No, well, you've been away at school so much until very lately, my love," replied her mother.

"Not *very* lately, Mama," corrected Anne, gently. "I left the Seminary eighteen months ago, you know."

"Is it as long as that?" asked Mrs. Hume, surprised.

"My, how the time goes on! It is time we were thinking of finding a husband for you, since you are past nineteen."

"That should present no difficulties," laughed Graham. "Who wouldn't be glad to take such an attractive miss, with all the housewifely virtues? I mustn't praise her physique on any account, you know," he added, slyly. "I've already been told by madam that I concentrate too much on people's physical attributes, and not enough on their higher selves."

Anne turned her face away from him, not daring to comment on this speech. She saw her mother looking at her closely, and to her annoyance felt a blush rising. She bent industriously over her work, hoping to hide it. Of course, he could not speak like that if he really meant anything by it. Evidently he was unaware, too, of certain expectations which had been entertained by her parents for the past few years. In a way, she wished that she herself had been likewise in ignorance; perhaps then she might not have lost her heart to him so readily. It was easy to see that to him she was still little Anne, six years his junior, whom he had teased and allowed to follow at his heels when he had been a happy-go-lucky schoolboy who had come to stay with them during the holidays. As she worked on his coat with patient fingers, she wondered if it would ever be in her power to make him see her as a woman whom he could desire for a wife.

He complimented her warmly on the

repair to his coat when he donned it on the following evening in readiness for his visit to Fulmer Towers. She thought wistfully that she had never seen him look so handsome. If the dark blue coat was a little tight over the shoulders, it only served to show off their breadth; and there was no fault to be found with the white waistcoat and black silk knee breeches, nor with the intricately tied cravat which completed the outfit. His crisp dark hair, which in general was allowed to become rumpled, had now been carefully groomed into the Roman style which was the current fashion.

She felt a sudden surge of pride in his appearance that was almost proprietorial. If only she might have had him as escort to some evening party or other, preferably not at Fulmer Towers.

Her face must have betrayed what she was feeling; for when the door had closed behind him Mrs. Hume put an arm about her daughter and said consolingly, "Never mind, my dear, it's only a visit of civility, after all."

6

Georgy Scores A Hit

AS Dr. Hume did not possess a carriage, his nephew was obliged to arrive at Fulmer Towers in the gig. The social ignominy of this did not strike him, so he found it no hardship; he was careless of such matters. When he arrived, he was shown into a small parlour where the men were sitting on their own, partaking of a glass of sherry wine before dinner. He was never more comfortable than when he was in male company, and was soon completely at home with all of them except Curshawe, whom he speedily set down as a prig and a bore. He could not help wondering how George Eversley, who even now frequently showed signs of impatience with Curshawe, would manage to tolerate the man as a brother-in-law.

Presently they were joined by the ladies. John Graham was surprised to see Georgiana in a wheel chair, and cast a quick, professional glance at her feet. Both her ankles were modestly covered, however, by the flounce of a simple gown in white muslin embroidered with tiny sprigs of forget-me-nots. A blue ribbon of the exact shade of the flowers was threaded through her tawny hair, which was arranged in seemingly artless curls. The whole effect was charming and unstudied; like most such effects, it had taken a great deal of time to achieve.

Yet another surprise was in store for him. She beckoned him to her side. As both Pamyngton and Curshawe had already taken up their stations one at each side of her wheel chair, he found himself part of a group when he obeyed her signal. She held out her hand to him, at the same time giving him a smile of such dazzling charm that he was quite taken aback.

"How do you do, Dr. Graham?" So far, he had never been privileged to hear such a soft, melodious tone to her voice. "I collect you called on my sister-in-law this morning. I am sorry to have missed you."

Obviously the other two men were as puzzled as he was by this volte-face. They stared at her in amazement and disbelief. The doctor was the first to recover. He gave a curt bow and one of his twisted smiles.

"I found Mrs. Eversley in excellent health," he said. "But I am sorry to see you are not yet able to stand. How is the ankle?"

"Oh, not as well as I could wish, sir. I would be grateful if you could take another look at it for me, later on."

"Certainly," he replied, with another short bow. "My services are at your disposal."

"It seems too bad to make you work on what ought to be an evening's relaxation," she said, apologetically, looking up at him from under her long lashes in a way that neither Pamyngton nor Curshawe could wholly approve, but which seemed to have very little effect upon Dr. Graham himself. "But if you could spare just a few moments after dinner? No one will be using this room then, so perhaps you could join me here? My maid will attend me."

82

"For all our sakes, Dr. Graham, I hope you'll not detain Miss Georgiana long," remarked Pamyngton, with a light laugh.

"Not five minutes, I imagine," returned Graham, carelessly. "Very well, ma'am, it shall be as you say."

He saw Georgy's green eyes flash. The next moment she was smiling graciously again, and he wondered if he could have been mistaken in thinking that something he said had made her angry.

The announcement of dinner was the signal for a polite wrangle to start up between Pamyngton and Curshawe as to who should have the honour of wheeling Georgiana into the dining-room. Growing tired of the argument, Freddy started forward and seized the handle himself.

"Oh, no!" exclaimed Georgy, with an exaggerated shudder of fear. "Not you, of all people!" She turned a coaxing look upon John Graham. "I think my medical adviser is the proper person for the duty."

"As you will, of course, ma'am," he agreed smoothly. He was frowning slightly as he pushed the chair along the passage and into the dining-room. Just what was she up to, this volatile young woman? Yesterday she had been ready to slit his throat, judging by her behaviour; and today she was all honey and mildness. It was possible, of course, that her behaviour yesterday had been the result of shock. Shock affected people in different ways; some went off into screaming fits, others were struck dumb, while a few would become aggressive and unreasonable, as Miss Eversley had done.

Even allowing for this, he could see no reason for her to show him such particular favour as she was treating him to at present. Women, of course, were notoriously subject to whims. He really knew very little about them, other than in a professional capacity. There had never seemed to be time in his life for becoming better acquainted with them as personalities.

He was taking no chances, however. He allowed two of the servants to assist Georgiana to her chair at the table, contenting himself with watching the proceedings with a keen, professional eye. At one point, he noticed that she actually put her foot to the ground and rested her weight on it without the least evidence of pain. His eyes narrowed: the suspicion crossed his mind that she was now quite able to use the injured foot if she chose. If so, what was her game?

He found himself sitting at table between Georgiana and Aunt Lavinia, with Pamyngton on Georgy's other side. For some time Pamyngton claimed most of Georgy's attention, and Graham was left to the polite small talk of Aunt Lavinia. But presently, Georgy turned towards him with one of the charming smiles that never failed to shatter her admirers.

"How do you find Buckinghamshire compares to your native Scotland, Dr. Graham?"

He hesitated. "One can't make a comparison, Miss Eversley. They are such very different types of country. Each, no doubt, has its admirers."

"I certainly can't judge," she said, fixing her lovely green eyes upon him in a way that he found slightly disconcerting.

"I have never been farther north than York."

"That is a pity." He smiled back at her with more ease than he felt. "Let me urge you to visit Edinburgh when you have the opportunity."

"I collect your home is in Edinburgh, then?"

He nodded. "Perhaps I am prejudiced on that account, but I think it as fine a town as London."

"Then I must certainly see it." How did she manage to get so much witchery into a smile? "But it will be of no use, you know, unless I am shown the town by one of its admirers. That is the only way to see anything to advantage."

"It seems hardly likely that the honour of showing it to you should fall to me," he replied, with a rueful smile that was not all politeness.

"But at least the spirit is willing," she said, with an arch look, "and I must thank you for that."

With this, she turned away to speak to Pamyngton on her other side; but as she did so, she flashed a look at her youngest brother, who was sitting opposite them at the table. He replied with a half-veiled wink which all at once fixed Graham's attention.

He frowned. Was this a normal brother and sister exchange, or were these two sharing a secret which was in some way connected with the conversation which had just taken place between Miss Eversley and himself, and which Freddy could easily have overheard if he chose? The idea seemed absurd, for they had said nothing beyond the usual trivialities of polite conversation. Yet the keen observation that was part of his calling insisted that there was a deeper significance in the look which brother and sister had shared.

She did not address him again for the duration of the meal. Perversely, he found himself hoping that she would. In the meantime, he was left with the view of a white shoulder turned away from him, and an opportunity to study the effect of candlelight on her richly tinted hair. Undoubtedly, he reflected, Miss Eversley was a very handsome woman: possibly she was not unaware of it, too.

After the meal was over, the gentlemen

did not sit very long over their wine. When they rose to join the ladies in the drawing-room, a footman summoned Dr. Graham to the small parlour where Georgiana was waiting in readiness to consult him about her injury.

After the door had closed upon the servant, Graham stood motionless by it for a moment. A feeling of unease began to creep over him. The room had been ablaze with light when they had occupied it before dinner. Now most of the candles had been snuffed, the only remaining light coming from the leaping fire and from a two-branched candlestand which stood on an occasional table close to where Georgiana was sitting. She was reclining in a wing-chair with her legs extended before her on a footstool; only the very tips of her blue kid sandals peeped modestly from under the flounce of her white gown. An abigail was by her side, a dark little Welsh girl with a demure face that did not match her saucy eyes. The pair of them, thought Graham with misgiving, looked ripe for mischief. His hand went instinctively to his cravat to straighten it, and he gave a light, professional cough.

"Well, now," he said, in what he hoped was a brisk manner. "Let's see what the trouble seems to be, shall we?"

The abigail hastily checked a titter, and was frowned on by her mistress. Graham went over to the chair, and stooped before the footstool. He put out his hands to seize a foot, then hesitated, looking up at the maid.

It was the first time he had ever felt ill at ease with a patient. He told himself that the unusual circumstances were to blame. It could not often fall to a young doctor's lot to be obliged to examine the ankle of an attractive young lady with whom he had just been chatting on the easiest of terms at a dinner party. Also the atmosphere in the room was wrong; all that shadow, and Miss Eversley sitting in a pool of mellow light, which made her hair glint as though it were a priceless jewel. He would have felt that she had deliberately arranged all this to put him at a disadvantage, but for the fact that there could be neither sense nor reason in such an action. Nevertheless, he could not avoid the uncomfortable feeling that both mistress and maid were laughing at him.

"If you'd be good enough to raise this hem a trifle," he commanded, a little more brusquely than the occasion seemed to justify.

The maid leant over to comply, obviously bubbling over with mirth. She had left her native valleys hoping to see a bit more life in London, and she had certainly not been disappointed since entering the Honourable Georgiana Eversley's service. Setting a good-looking young doctor on to examine an ankle that was as good as ever, look you, was only one of the many pranks that could be expected from her handsome, harum scarum mistress — and good luck to her, yes, indeed, for were not the men there to be bamboozled? She would have something worth the telling when next she made the long, uncomfortable journey back to her birthplace.

"That will do, thank you," said Graham, sharply, as the girl twitched the flounce of her mistress's gown well above the ankle. "Now, let me see, it's this one, isn't it?"

His vague suspicions prompted him to feign a mistake; it was the left ankle, and not the right, which he took in his hands.

"There's no swelling," he said, moving his fingers gently over the affected area. He pressed hard suddenly, and looked up at Georgy with a bland expression of inquiry on his face. "Does that hurt?" he asked.

She nodded and gave a small sigh, then put up a hand to her head.

"Stevens," she said, in a failing voice, "I think I may need my vinaigrette. Will you fetch it, please?"

"Indeed to goodness, madam, I hope you may not swoon!" exclaimed Stevens with a great show of alarm, making a bolt for the door.

"Have no fear — while Dr. Graham is with me, I can come to no harm," Georgy assured her, weakly. "Only I should feel more comfortable with my smelling bottle."

"Yes, to be sure, Miss — I will fetch it instantly!"

The door closed behind her. Graham released the foot, and rose to his feet.

"I imagine you'd prefer me to postpone the rest of the examination until your maid returns," he said, brusquely. "By the way, if you really feel faint, put your head forward — so!"

He caught hold of her by the shoulders, and jerked her forward so suddenly that the pins which held her back hair in place were loosened, and it came tumbling about her neck in a tawny mass of ringlets.

She shook herself free of his grip, and turned her flashing green eyes upon him.

"How dare you?" she blazed.

"And how dare you?" he retaliated. "Let me inform you that I was holding your *left* ankle, whereas it was your right which you strained. I pity your sufferings, indeed, if you can't even tell the difference!"

"Oh!" For a moment, she looked seriously taken aback. Then she made a quick recovery. "Well, whichever it was, it did hurt most vilely, for you were very rough with it!"

"Not as rough as I would like to be," he said, grimly. "Allow me to tell you, madam, that there's nothing whatever wrong with either of your ankles, and you may walk on them whenever you've a mind to do so."

"How do you know that?" she demanded, indignantly. "You haven't so much as looked at the injured one, as yet!"

"I've seen enough to judge. There's no swelling or bruising — moreover, I observed that when you came to table, you could very well have used it, had you wished."

"How dare you!" she repeated, fiercely. "You are insufferable!"

He laughed shortly. "Come, this is better, isn't it? This is more in your usual vein! I thought it might have been the shock to your system which made you so vastly disagreeable the other day, but now I see it is your natural state, after all. I can't pretend to guess why it has pleased you to treat me with so much civility and charm this evening; but I'll wager it's for some purpose of your own, and not just the politeness you feel is due to a guest. You are not likely to concern yourself with such things."

"Nor are you, it seems!"

"I am the guest, not yourself. Is this your notion of hospitality in England — to play off hoaxes on those who are so unfortunate or misguided as to find themselves under your roof? 'Pon my soul, you might be any schoolroom hoyden, instead of — " He stopped abruptly.

"Instead of what?" she demanded, with chilling dignity.

"No matter! It's all of a piece, I suppose. Females of your standing in the world have no rational worthwhile occupation, so they are reduced to passing their tedious hours in buffoonery of this kind."

"A hoyden, a buffoon," she repeated, dangerously calm. "Pray have you any more graceful compliments to pay me, doctor?"

For a moment he stared in silence at the lovely face with its arrogantly tilted chin and blazing green eyes, framed by the tumbled red-gold curls. He drew in his breath sharply.

"No. I have done," he replied, harshly.

The door opened while he was still

standing there staring down at her, and Stevens entered, clutching the vinaigrette.

"Here it is, madam. I couldn't find it at first." She unstoppered the bottle, and held it under Georgy's nose, her lips quivering with suppressed mirth. "There, how do you feel now, Miss Georginia?"

Georgy waved the bottle away. "I feel capital, thank you, Stevens. But I think perhaps you should offer the bottle to Dr. Graham."

7

Freddy Is Optimistic

JOHN GRAHAM did not stay long after his interview with Georgy. He was hailed as a miracle-worker when she walked unaided into the drawingroom a little ahead of him; but her slightly flushed face told Beau Eversley, at any rate, that the miracle had failed to please her. He discussed it with Susan later on, in the privacy of her bedchamber. She was leaning back against the pillows, attired in a demure nightgown of white lawn, with her dark hair loosely tied back from her face by a knot of pink ribbon.

He took her hand, and pressed it to his lips before clasping it in both his own as he sat beside her on the bed.

"You look weary, my own," he said, gently.

She gave him the soft confiding smile that he often saw on baby Maria's small face.

"A little," she acknowledged. "I'm so heavy and clumsy these days, everything takes more energy than it used to do."

"You're quite sure that you feel no ill effects from that abominable escapade of Georgy's?" he asked, solicitously. "I know that George's medico friend is confident no harm has been done, and he seems a sound enough chap — " He broke off, frowning ominously. "I may tell you, Sue, I could cheerfully have throttled that girl when I thought of the risk in which she involved you! I gave her a thorough dressing down this morning; let's hope it did some good."

"Poor Georgy!" replied his wife, with a sigh. "She didn't mean any harm, you know, Hugh. But she suddenly takes a notion into her head, and nothing will do but she must carry it out, with never a thought of the consequences. I understand her — after all, I was once just the same myself, as I needn't tell you, dearest."

"No, you were not," he said, with energy. "Oh, yes, you were impetuous, and perhaps given" — he softened the criticism with a smile — "to occasional flights of fancy, shall we say?" He pressed her imprisoned hand, and leaned forward to kiss her lightly on the tip of her nose. "But you were never so wild and outrageous as Georgy. She gets up to the most hare-brained starts for absolutely no reason at all that anyone can see. And it isn't even as if she were too young and naïve to realize the outcome of her larks, as you were then — why, you were scarce eighteen when I married you. But Georgy is turned one-and-twenty, and as well up to snuff as anyone, when she chooses. Damned if I know what ails the girl? Evelina was nothing like the same trouble. But there we are — she's headstrong, and my father indulges her. If mother had lived, it would have been a different story. She could always manage Georgy all right."

"I don't think," said Sue, doubtfully, "that she's really very happy, you know, Hugh."

"Why should she not be happy?" he demanded, incredulously. "She has everything she could want; health, fortune, rank, friends and admirers — no wonder they call her the Toast of the Town, for some misguided man or other is always at her heels. Added to which, she already has an establishment of her own without having to call any man master in order to get it — "

"Perhaps that is the trouble," said Susan, with a wise look which had the effect of making her appear more childlike. "Perhaps she would be happier if she had a husband to master her."

He laughed. "Let me tell you, I wouldn't envy him the task. She's been unschooled for too long. Breaking her to the bit will be a job for a very patient, not to say practised, hand."

"Well, and I think there might be someone not very far away who could do it," said Susan, mysteriously.

He raised one eyebrow at her, a mannerism of his which she found irresistible. "You do, eh? Do you mean to tell me who this conqueror is?"

"Lord Pamyngton," she answered simply.

He pursed his lips consideringly. "Pam? Yes, perhaps. Certainly madam treats him with slightly more respect than she accords to most of her admirers. But does Pam intend marriage? And, if he does, would Georgy accept him?"

"You must be a better judge of his intentions than I can pretend to be, dearest. After all, he is a friend of yours."

"Well, yes — Peter Radley sees more of him than I do, in fact, but I doubt if even he is in Pam's confidence on that score. However, judging from what I know of Pam, I would say he's very smitten with Georgy, but doesn't mean to wear his heart on his sleeve. Perhaps that's why Georgy does not use him so abominably as she does some of her other admirers! Sometimes I wonder she has any left, from what I see of her cavalier treatment of them."

"She does lead them a dance at times," admitted Susan, with a laugh. "But she has such a deal of natural, unstudied charm that it robs her words and actions of any offence. And she is so lovely, Hugh! When she comes into a room, you can see every gentleman there sitting up and taking notice. Her admirers are quite ready to overlook a little liveliness of disposition that may at times seem to

100

take a delight in tormenting them."

Beau Eversley frowned. "Do you know what her feelings are for Pam? I imagine she would confide in you, if she would in anybody."

"She has said nothing, and I haven't taxed her with questions," replied Susan, shaking her head. "But I know Georgy, and I can see that she likes him more than all the rest put together. Sometimes I think that it needs something — a crisis of some kind, though I wouldn't for the world wish either of them any misfortune, to be sure! — but some event which would show them what they mean to each other. Just as you and I, dearest, needed to be shown the way to our happiness — remember?"

"Shall I ever forget?" He leaned forward and took her into his arms.

For a time, there was silence in the room.

"Hugh," said Susan, at length, drawing a little away from him, "why do you suppose Georgy was pretending this evening that her ankle was worse than it really was? She was walking on it well enough this morning when she came into my bedchamber while I was drinking my chocolate. She said then that she scarce felt a twinge. Yet this evening she came into the room in the wheel chair, and asked the doctor to take a look at it — " she broke off, and sighed. "I must confess it puzzled me no end; but, of course, I said nothing to betray her, for I suppose I must have been the only one who saw her walking on it, and I would not for worlds divulge anything that she wished to keep secret! But what could she mean by it? Have you any notion?"

"Oh, the devil take my sister!" exclaimed Hugh, drawing his wife close again. "We've talked of her for quite long enough. I've no thought to spare for any other woman than you, my sweet and only love!"

★ ★ ★

"He bubbled you, then," said Freddy, listening on the following morning to Georgiana's light-hearted account of her interview with Dr. Graham. "Pity. It would have made a capital excuse for bringing you together, if only you could have made him believe the ankle pained you, and needed constant attention. Too much to expect, though, that a competent medico could be so taken in, unless it suited his book to pretend he was. And our Dr. Graham" — he chuckled — "doesn't dote on you to the extent that he's glad of any excuse to call on you. No, sister, you've a deal of hard work to put in there, I promise you! You're at a bit of a stand, now, my dear — reckon I'll win this wager, damme if I don't."

"Don't count your chickens!" retorted Georgy, with spirit. "You must think me a very poor creature, if you don't suppose I shall contrive to throw myself in the dear doctor's way. Besides, George wants to see something of him while he is down here, so I can reasonably expect that he will be visiting us quite often — and then he will be calling in on Susan occasionally, in the way of duty. Oh, it won't be too difficult! I think I'll suggest to Susan that she should give a ball," she added, thoughtfully. "There's nothing like dancing to bring people together, and provide opportunities for a little dalliance."

"Well, I will wish you luck, Georgy, for I think you'll need it!" scoffed Freddy, as he left her. "Your blunt's as good as in my pocket already, in my view!"

Privately, Georgiana thought so herself. It was plain that Dr. Graham was not going to be such a ready victim as she had at first supposed. She had come to accept her undoubted power over men in no boastful spirit, but as one of the facts of existence. They had always flocked to her side without any conscious effort on her part to attract them; so it had never occurred to her to doubt her ability to succeed with any man whom she deliberately set out to please. It was a shock to discover that she was wrong, but she did not despair. Instead, she blamed her tactics. Evidently she had been too obvious. She had made the mistake of underestimating her quarry.

But although the doctor had resisted her attempts at entangling him, she knew that he had not remained entirely impervious to her feminine appeal. Her quick perception sensed that she had awakened some masculine reaction, although obviously he had no intention of giving it rein.

What was to be done now? The one thing she was quite determined against was to abandon the chase. The difficulties had only added a stronger sporting element to the wager with Freddy. Besides, she wanted to bring the man to his knees, she told herself fiercely. He had insulted and mocked her, he had dared to deride where others could do nothing but admire . . .

If only she understood his character better, her task might be easier. Most people had a vulnerable point that could be played upon. Although she herself had always scorned such tricks, she had watched other females at them often enough, especially in their dealings with men. Some men could never resist the flattery of wide-eyed innocents who hung on their every word in wonder; others would more readily succumb to the appeal of a helpless, clinging female who made a great play of needing a strong arm to support her. She had seen such bait offered countless times, and swallowed nearly as often, she thought contemptuously. And was she not about to indulge in such despicable antics herself? She smiled cynically, looking for a moment very like her brother Hugh. At least, she consoled herself, it was revenge and not vanity that prompted her to do what in truth went very much against the grain. Perhaps George would be able to throw some light on his friend's character. But no! George was certainly not one to analyse his fellow man. To use his own terms, Graham was a very good sort of chap, and that was enough for George. Besides, she had no wish to arouse her brother's curiosity by showing any particular interest in his friend. It would never do for George to learn of the wager between herself and Freddy. There seemed nothing to be done at present but to await the next time when she and the doctor would be thrown together, and to make the best use she could of their meeting.

After two days had gone by without any such encounter taking place, she began to feel impatient. She had barely three weeks in which to make her conquest, and she had not even made a beginning.

If events would not happen of their own accord, then she must make them happen. But how? Feverishly, she evolved plans whenever she had a moment's solitude.

Solitude was not easy to find at present. Some scheme for the day was always afoot — walking, driving, or else visiting the neighbouring gentry. Sometimes the whole party went on these expeditions, sometimes there was one plan for the ladies and another for the gentlemen. It rarely happened that Georgy found herself alone except in the privacy of her bed-chamber. This frustration tended at times to make her thoughtful in company.

Pamyngton taxed her with it on one occasion.

The whole party was returning from a call on a neighbour who lived only a short distance away. Georgy had managed to avoid being shut up in the family carriage, choosing instead to ride with Pamyngton in his curricle, which he had brought down with him from London. Curshawe, who had not had the forethought to bring his own vehicle to Fulmer Towers, was obviously very put out by her choice, and inclined to sulk.

He himself was on horseback, and took every opportunity of riding beside them and sharing their conversation, which was inclined to be spasmodic owing to Georgy's abstraction.

"Perhaps," said Pamyngton, with a sigh, "you don't agree with my observation, and that is why you keep silent."

Georgy started, conscious of having been addressed before, but not having the faintest notion of what had been said to her. "I beg your pardon — I didn't quite catch what you said."

"No," he agreed, with a gently teasing smile. "My voice, I realize, is not of any great power. And we are sitting so far apart, of course."

She laughed. "Oh, Pam, you are absurd! I must confess I was thinking of something else. What did you say to me?"

"Nothing of any great momentum. Some observations on the scenery, which no doubt you will find done rather better in one of the poets. But I would like to know," he added, "what inspires so much deep thought in you, Miss Georgy?" He stared ahead at the horses for a moment.

"Can anything be troubling you? If so, perhaps I could be of assistance? I am always yours to command, you know."

His tone was quite light, but she sensed a deeper feeling behind it that slightly embarrassed her for a moment.

"Oh, no! It was nothing — sometimes one day-dreams — " He turned towards her, and she looked hastily away from the deep blue eyes.

"As you say," he replied quietly. "But I should not have supposed that you were much afflicted with that malady."

She did not quite know how to answer, but she was saved the effort by Curshawe, who had once more drawn alongside them.

"What malady is Miss Georgiana afflicted with, Pamyngton?" he asked, in a loud, bright tone. "She'd best consult that doctor fellow, hadn't she?" He laughed unconvincingly, then gestured ahead with his whip. "Talk of the devil! If I'm not much mistaken, here he comes, too!"

They both looked ahead and saw the doctor's gig approaching. Georgy's face at once took on more animation.

"We must stop for a moment," she

said, quickly, "just to have a word with him."

"As you wish," said Pamyngton, studying her face thoughtfully.

He reined in the horses as they drew abreast of the gig, and called out a cheerful good day. But it seemed that Dr. Graham was in a hurry. He doffed his hat, bowed, returned the greeting with a polite smile, called out "Sorry, can't stop — on my way to a case," and passed them in a whirl of dust.

"Well, really!" exclaimed Curshawe, when the gig was well past and still travelling at what must have been the limit of poor old Nelly's powers. "One would have thought common civility might have made the fellow pull up and pay his respects to you, Miss Eversley."

"Oh, come," said Pamyngton, mildly. "He might be on his way to a death bed, you know."

Curshawe made some reply, but Georgy did not hear what it was, for she was deep in thought again.

Pamyngton noticed this with misgiving.

8

The Rescue

GEORGY retired to bed that night with her head full of half-fledged schemes that seemed, on closer scrutiny, to be feeble in the extreme. Yawning widely, she dropped off to sleep at last on the wondering thought that no wager in the world was worth half the trouble she was taking over this one.

Surprisingly, she awoke with a clear mind and the certainty of what she meant to do. This was no less than to eat humble pie for Dr. Graham's benefit; she intended to apologize to the gentleman for the jest she had played upon him the other evening.

In general, only a very strong conviction of being in the wrong would ever induce Georgiana Eversley to apologize to anyone. She certainly did not feel any such conviction over her behaviour towards John Graham; in her view, it had been fully justified by his previous conduct towards her. But a graceful apology seemed to her the quickest way of putting them on the kind of terms that would forward her purpose. He could not be so churlish as to spurn her efforts to make amends.

She jumped out of bed and looked at the clock, surprised to see that it was only half past six. Sweeping back the curtain from the window, she looked out on a grey sky that was still streaked with the pink tints of dawn. Her resolution hardened. There was no time like the present; she would go and see Dr. Graham now, while no one else in the house was astir. She paused for a moment, wondering if he, too, would still be in bed, fast asleep; but finally decided that most likely doctors, like domestic servants, had to be up early in the morning.

She dressed carefully in a becoming lavender walking dress and a bonnet trimmed with ribbons of the same shade. Lavender, so she had been told, gave her a demure look — what could be better for making an apology, and helping to soften a hard heart? The servants were already busy at their work on the ground floor of the house, but she did not trouble them for any breakfast. One or two stared after her as she made her way to the front door, and the housemaid who was busy scrubbing the steps leapt up in a startled way when she appeared. Apart from the domestics, she met no one.

It was not far to the village; Georgy enjoyed the exercise on such a fine morning. She sniffed the crisp, clear air appreciatively as she walked between fields where cattle were grazing peacefully or where reapers were hard at work stooking the ripe corn. She thought how beautiful the trees looked in their autumn dress of amber, gold and red. Trees were always beautiful; from their first green beginnings in the Spring to the time when they shook the last of the tawny leaves from their heads to stand stark and black against the sky, waiting for the softening touch of snow. She smiled to find her thoughts taking such a poetic turn. It was scarcely the occasion for it, she reminded herself.

The first barns and cottages came into

view and before long she was walking along the main street of the village. Here everyone was stirring; housewives were shaking mats before their doors, a girl was driving a small flock of geese towards the village green, and the village butcher was sharpening a knife on the step of his shop. Nearly everyone looked up curiously as she passed, and most of them gave her good morning. She responded graciously to these greetings, and walked on with outward nonchalance, but mounting inward trepidation, towards Dr. Hume's house.

It stood almost at the end of the street, close to the point where the main coach road skirted the village — Georgy's step slowed as she approached it, until she finally came to a halt outside, staring at the windows. All she gained from this was the sight of fresh, white dimity curtains, and a bowl of red and yellow chrysanthemums standing on one of the lower window sills. There was no sign of life.

She hesitated, nerving herself to open the gate and approach the house. It was surprising to discover that what had seemed such a simple thing to do when she had started on her walk, should prove so difficult at the end of it. It was not only surprising; it was humiliating. She rated herself inwardly, but still lacked the courage to stretch her hand out to the latch of the gate.

Well, she could not stand here for ever; before long someone must notice her, and wonder why in the world she was dawdling at the doctor's gate. She turned away, and walked slowly on to the junction of the village street with the coach road. Two women were standing gossiping outside the gate of the end cottage, while a toddler played at their feet, scooping up handfuls of the brightly coloured leaves which lay on the ground. So intent were they on their gossip that they took no notice whatever of Georgy, much to her relief. She walked past them, turned into the main road, and then halted at a point where the end wall of the cottage shut her off from their view.

She would not abandon her plan, she told herself fiercely. She certainly had not dressed herself with such care and walked all this way at such an unseasonable hour of day, only to walk tamely back with her mission unaccomplished. She could never live with herself if she should weakly submit to such craven conduct. The sound of a vehicle approaching at speed along the road to London beat out a hurried rhythm to her thoughts. She must return now — at once, with no more dallying — to Dr. Hume's house, and ring the bell.

She flung back her head with a proud gesture, and turned to retrace her steps.

At that moment, the London-bound Mail Coach came hurtling down the road in a flurry of wheels, hoofs and jingling harness, and a defiant blast from the guard's horn. As it neared the road junction, a small toddler who had followed Georgy unheeded ran with unsteady steps right into its path.

★ ★ ★

Afterwards, Georgiana could never say with any certainty what followed. Every other thought dropped away from her but the one instinctive maternal urge to protect — she plunged after the child and scooped it up in her arms. It struggled, bawling loudly. Suddenly there was a hullabaloo all about her. The Mail Coach men shouted and swore as the driver strained every nerve to bring his horses to a standstill in time to avoid running down Georgiana and the child. The two women who had been gossiping as if nothing could stop them only a short while since, now stood whitefaced and screaming at the side of the road. The noise brought men from the fields, and people from their houses to the street, where they stood huddled together in frightened groups, watching.

In spite of all this noise, Georgy kept her head. Clutching the child with difficulty, for it struggled wildly to escape restraint, she ran as hard as she could out of the path of the oncoming vehicle. Her skirt caught under her foot. She heard it tear, and plunged on, panting in her efforts to control the child. The skirt caught a second time — she tripped, recovered, then finally stumbled, measuring her length upon the ground. As she fell, she threw the child clear of the approaching danger.

With a loud screeching of brakes and a frightened whinnying of horses, the Mail Coach came to a standstill barely a foot from where Georgiana was lying, partly stunned by her fall.

After that, everything was even more confused. The child, unhurt save for a few bruises, was bellowing wildly. Its frightened mother gathered it to her bosom and began a hysterical wailing of her own. The passengers and guard dismounted from the Mail and formed a now rapidly growing crowd which gathered about her. Shouts, wails, a hubbub of voices — she shut her eyes tightly, and wished they would all go away.

"What's going on here? Make way!"

Dimly she recognized the voice of command that rang out above the hubbub, but she was too dazed to put a name to its owner. She heard the quick fire of questions from the same voice, and a babble of answers from members of the crowd. And then she was trying to sit up, and ready hands were helping her to her feet. She stood swaying between two men when the crowd parted, and a figure stood before her that seemed familiar, but had a regrettable tendency to sway from side to side.

"Good God, Miss Eversley!" exclaimed the newcomer. "So it was you! Can you tell me how you are hurt?"

She shook her head. "I fell," she answered, simply.

His eyes went quickly to her right arm. There was a rent in her sleeve above the elbow, and blood was staining it.

"We'll see to that," he said, briskly. "No bones broken, I think, but we'd best make sure." After a pause, "All right, you two, I'll carry the lady to my surgery."

Georgiana opened her lips to say that she was very well able to walk there on her own two feet, but the words seemed to involve too much effort. Something must have shown in her face, for he said, gently again: "You must forgive me, but it's the best way. You're as game as they come, but you're feeling none too steady at present, are you?"

The men released her, and for the second time recently, he took her up in his arms. His manner was very different from what it had been on that first occasion, however: now he handled her as if she were made of some fragile substance.

"The lady *is* a game one, and no mistake, sir," said one of the men who had helped Georgy to her feet. "I saw her from the field yonder" — he waved his hand in the direction of the road — "she rushed out into the road straight in front o' the Mail after the little nipper, wi' never a thought o' danger. And there's some who'd a better call to do what she done, too, an' them not so far away at that, wi' their tongues aclacking, as usual!"

There was a murmur of approbation from the crowd, that swelled to a cheer as Graham moved through it with his burden towards Dr. Hume's house.

Georgy raised her face to his. The mists were clearing from her mind, and now she felt a surge of anxiety.

"The child!" she exclaimed, distractedly. "Is it all right? Oh, pray see to it, and do not trouble with me!"

"Don't concern yourself," he replied, in a soothing tone, as they reached the

120

door, which was standing ajar. "I've already taken a look at the child, and it's sustained no hurt but a bruise and a scrape or two. No child bawls in that lusty way when it's seriously injured."

He broke off, to address his aunt and cousin, who were standing in the doorway with dismayed and anxious faces. "Don't be alarmed — this lady isn't much hurt. Cousin Anne, I shall need your good offices. Some warm water, if you please, to the surgery. And I think perhaps, Aunt, a hot cup on tea might not come amiss. Now, Miss Eversley!"

He swept into the surgery with her, laying her gently down on a day-bed which was over by the window.

"I think perhaps," he said, in the same quiet tone he had used to her from the moment he had taken her up in his arms, "we shall need to spoil this pretty gown by cutting the sleeve. Do you mind very much?"

Georgy was feeling much more steady now. She gave him a shaky smile. "Not a jot — it's already quite ruined." She put up hands which trembled slightly, and discovered that her bonnet had fallen back from her head and was dangling by its strings. "What a sight I must look!" she added, ruefully.

He ignored this, producing a pair of scissors and carefully cutting away the sleeve of her gown from the wound beneath. While he was doing this, Anne entered the room carrying a bowl of water which she set down close at hand. She then fetched some bandages and pots of ointment from a cupboard, and stood waiting patiently at Graham's side while he examined the wound.

"I think you must have cut this on a jagged stone as you fell," he said. "It's not too bad, though. Once we've cleaned it up, it should be quite satisfactory."

"I don't call anything satisfactory," said Georgy, with an uncertain smile, "that makes such a prodigious mess!"

"Soon take care of that," he assured her. "Now, this may hurt a little — "

While he cleaned and bandaged the wound, Georgy covertly studied his assistant. She had not realized that Dr. Hume had a daughter, and an attractive one at that; but hearing Dr. Graham call the young lady cousin, she knew there could be no mistake. Miss Hume was small and dainty, with grave brown eyes and soft brown hair that framed an oval face. She moved without fuss or bustle, yet gave an impression of quiet efficiency that Georgy could see at once fitted very well in a sick room. Just such a girl would make an excellent wife for a doctor, Georgy found herself thinking; although it was unheard of for a gently-reared female to do any professional nursing, of course. Professional female nurses were not only rough and untutored as a general rule, but all too often gin-sodden into the bargain. Midwives in particular tended to be of the latter kind, and it was shocking to think of the numbers of fashionable women who still entrusted the delivery of their babies to such creatures. Thank goodness Hugh had more enlightened ideas, and had followed the Royal example in engaging a doctor to bring his and Susan's children into the world. There had been many who had questioned his choice of a humble country doctor, though, and had wondered why he had not sought the services of one of the fashionable 'man-midwives', as doctors were called who specialized in confinement cases. But Dr. Hume had a sound reputation in that part of Buckinghamshire, and Susan preferred to pass most of her time in the country when she was pregnant. It was better, so Hugh had decided, to settle for someone who lived close at hand. His choice had been amply justified when their first child had been born, and now Susan awaited her second confinement with every confidence in Dr. Hume's ministrations. All the same, reflected Georgy, it must be most useful for any doctor to have a quiet, efficient helpmeet such as Anne Hume at hand; one who could be relied upon to supply intelligent, skilful assistance when required, and yet would not be so sensitive that she would swoon at the mere sight of blood.

Her eyes travelled from Miss Hume's face to Graham's. He had almost finished now, and was about to secure the bandage. He was intent on what he was doing, his deft fingers moving with a practised skill, so he did not notice her scrutiny. His touch inspired confidence, thought Georgy; here was a man who not only knew what he was doing, but who also seemed to know that this was the only work he wanted to be doing in the world. A little ironical smile twisted her lips for a moment, giving her a fleeting resemblance to her brother Hugh. If the doctor had both a vocation for his work, and a female in view who would be willing and able to assist him in it, then no wonder he had found it easy to resist the charms of the so-called irresistible Georgiana Eversley. So much for her wager with Freddy. She had better call it off.

"There, that's finished," said Graham, straightening up and smiling down at her. "Now how do you feel, ma'am?"

She flashed an answering smile. "Splendidly, I thank you."

"Capital! Then I think we'll transfer you to the parlour, where a hot drink is most likely waiting for you, by now. I'll carry you there — with your permission."

"But I ought to be returning home," protested Georgy. "No one has the slightest notion where I may be. I slipped out before the others were astir."

"Would you like me to send someone with a message? You should rest here for a while, you know, until you are feeling more the thing. Then I'll take you home in the gig — although most likely they'll send a carriage for you from the Towers, if we let them know what has happened."

"No!" exclaimed Georgy, remembering something. "If you send a message saying I am hurt, it may upset Susan. They won't worry about my absence unduly — sometimes I go riding before breakfast."

"What a strange mixture you are!" he said, involuntarily. "You can think of Mrs. Eversley's welfare at a time like this, when you are in some pain and discomfort yourself — and yet you never spared her a thought the other day, when you were entirely bent on your own pleasure!"

"It is not at all the same thing!" replied Georgy, with a flash of spirit. "And it is very ungallant of you to remind me of — of a past error! I think you may take me home at once. Thank you for your ministrations."

She attempted to swing her legs off the couch on to the floor, but he stopped her, shaking his head.

"You're quite right, and I apologize," he said, with a smile that reached his dark eyes. "Come, we shall not quarrel at present — let me take you into the parlour to my aunt. Afterwards, we can decide whether or not to send a message to your brother."

He bent to raise her gently in his arms, and she made no move to prevent him. As he carried her through the door which Anne held open for him, his eyes lingered for a moment on the tawny head which rested against his shoulder. A disconcertingly unprofessional feeling suddenly took hold of him. It showed in his eyes for a moment as he passed by his cousin. Anne Hume followed him into the parlour with a sinking heart.

9

Two In A Gig

ALTHOUGH Georgiana would have been reluctant to admit it, she had been shaken by her recent experience; but she had an excellent constitution and soon felt completely herself again, apart from the dull ache of the wound in her arm. While she chatted easily to Mrs. Hume and her daughter over a cup of tea, she began to debate inwardly whether or not to let Dr. Graham drive her home.

Her first thought on seeing him with Miss Hume had been to abandon the wager between herself and Freddy. It seemed all too likely that there must be some thought of marriage between the two cousins. But now she was not so sure. She studied them keenly but unobtrusively as she took part in the normal interchange of polite conversation; and after half an hour or so in their

128

company she was ready to lay another wager, had there been anyone of a sporting turn handy to accept it. While Anne Hume gave many little evidences, unmistakable to a feminine eye, of a strong partiality towards her handsome cousin, Graham himself showed no obvious sign of reciprocating it. It was easy to see that he was fond of Anne. He treated her with a careless affection that to Georgy's eyes had more of the brother than the lover about it. Possibly, thought Georgy, little Miss Hume was hoping that time would improve on this. She was an attractive female, and they were living under the same roof, constantly thrown together for company. Well; she could have him — that was to say, if she could get him — after Georgiana Eversley had done with him. He must first bow the knee before the Incomparable, the Toast of the Town.

Having made up her mind on this, Georgy shook her head when Graham asked her again if he should send a message to Fulmer Towers for someone to come and collect her.

"If you can truly spare the time, I

think I will accept your kind offer to convey me home yourself," she replied with a winning smile. "If Mrs. Eversley sees me well and strong before her eyes, she cannot worry; but a message saying that I've had an accident might frighten her out of her wits."

"As to the time, why, Fulmer Towers is on my way to a call I must make this morning." His face clouded for a moment. "The only thing is, we have no vehicle but the gig, and I fear you won't find it too comfortable, with your arm as it is." He paused, considering. "Of course, I could walk the mare — it isn't far — and then I shan't crowd you."

"No such thing!" exclaimed Georgy. "I shall contrive to keep my arm out of your way." She put down her cup, and rose to her feet unaided for the first time since entering the doctor's house.

"How do you feel?" he asked, watching her face.

"Yes, indeed, ma'am, have a care!" warned Mrs. Hume, rising also, and coming to Georgy's side. "You have had a nasty shock, you know!"

Georgy nodded, smiling. "But I am

quite recovered, now, thanks to your kind offices, ma'am, and those of your daughter and nephew. I am quite able to go home, and I think I ought to go at once. It will not do to put everyone in a bustle, wondering where I am."

Seeing that her mind was made up, Graham had the gig brought round from the stable, and Georgy took her leave of his aunt and cousin, once again thanking them for their ministrations in her usual frank, sincere style.

The young doctor handed her up into the gig carefully before seating himself beside her. He took up the reins, and slow, fat Nelly began to amble placidly down the village street in the direction of Fulmer Towers.

There was silence between them at first. As the last of the cottages was left behind, Graham turned towards her to ask how she was feeling now.

"Oh, splendidly, thank you!" She gave a rueful little laugh, and held up the bedraggled bonnet which she was dangling from one hand. "I only wish I could say the same of this — what a poor wreck it's become, to be sure!"

"We must be thankful that you didn't fare as badly," he replied, with an answering grin. "Another foot or so, and those horses would have trampled you."

"Oh, well, it didn't happen," she said, airily. "The Mail coachmen are pretty fair drivers, are they not?"

"You are a judge of driving, of course," he ventured, his grin broadening.

He saw a flash of anger in her eyes, but it vanished in a moment. She laughed readily enough. "Well, you may not think so, but the fact is that I *am* considered a tolerable whip, even by my brothers — though they usually add the words 'for a female' to any compliment they may pay me on my driving."

"Naturally. One wouldn't expect the same standards to apply."

"Why not?" There was no mistaking the spark in those green eyes now.

"It's largely a matter of physique. Men have stronger hands than women, for one thing."

"Oh, stuff!" she said, impatiently. "What has that to say to anything? A daintier wrist than mine may acquire strength through practice!"

"That's true enough, of course." He glanced at her wrists. Her gloves were as soiled and torn as her bonnet, and she had discarded them. "I suppose there may be daintier wrists than yours, since you seem to think so," he added, spontaneously.

She laughed, and tossed her tangled auburn curls. "Oh, it will never do for you to be paying me compliments! I thought we were agreed that it is to be war to the knife between us!"

"No such thing. I have no wish to quarrel with you, Miss Eversley. That was a very brave thing you did — the child would most likely have been killed had you not been there, and kept your wits about you."

She coloured a little. "Oh, it was nothing — anyone would have done the same!"

He shook his head. "I can't agree. And it was an especially brave thing for a female — "

She interrupted him with a contemptuous laugh. "There you go again! Pray, why should you consider it a braver thing for a woman than for a man?"

"Because they are more timid by nature, less likely to plunge into action without weighing the physical consequences — "

"Oh, pooh!" exclaimed Georgiana, in disgust. "What fustian you do gabble, to be sure! Let me tell you, Dr. Graham, that all your medical training hasn't succeeded in teaching you the first little thing about women!"

"That may well be true," he acknowledged, slowly. "I seldom encounter any, except in a professional way. In fact, only the other day my cousin Anne was saying to me," he went on half to himself, "that I have a tendency to think of the people I meet only in physical terms, and not to take sufficient account of their characters, thoughts and feelings."

"Believe me, she's not far wrong," replied Georgy, emphatically. She made a mental note that evidently Miss Hume could not feel too certain of her cousin's affections, since she talked to him in this vein. "But one thing I can plainly see — however small your acquaintance with females may be, it has given you no great opinion of the sex as a whole."

Graham opened his mouth to deny this, then shut it again. "It would be against all my training," he said, at length, "to speak of what I do not know."

"It won't serve you to hedge," said Georgy, laughing, "your attitude is only too plain. Now why, I wonder? Why should you have such a poor opinion of us?"

"You're pitching it too strong," he replied, joining in her laughter. "I only say of women what I have observed in my work — that they are physically weaker than men and less liable to take violent action. What possible objection can you make to that?"

"Oh, but it's not only that! It's a kind of superiority that you adopt whenever you mention us — as though we were beneath serious consideration!"

He whistled. "Do I?" he asked, in mock consternation. "You must blame my lack of address on the cause that I mentioned to you before. Apart from patients, I have spent scarcely any time in female company for the past two years or more."

135

"There is your cousin, Miss Hume," she pointed out. "And have you no sister, nor a mother?"

"Oh, yes," he answered, "but they are in Scotland, and my visits home have been all too few for many years now. As for Anne, I've seen very little of her since she grew up, until just lately. Besides," he added, suddenly, "sisters and cousins are not at all the same thing."

She shot a provocative glance at him out of her green eyes. "No?"

He shook his head. "One takes one's family for granted in a way that isn't possible with other people. They're like a familiar countryside which, though loved, has nothing new to offer the explorer."

"Well expressed, sir! I see that the man of science has a poetic streak, after all!"

He laughed. "Perhaps. After all, I was originally intended for the Church, you know. My father is a clergyman himself, and sent me to Oxford with that in view."

She was interested. "What made you change your mind?"

He hesitated. "I was never really set on the Church — I think it was the frequent holidays I spent down here in Buckinghamshire with my uncle that first turned my thoughts to the medical profession. Whenever I came here as a lad, I used to go round with him in the gig when he was making his calls, and sometimes I was allowed to watch him at work on the simpler cases. I fell in with my father's plans for my future in the way that sons often do, however, without thinking overmuch for myself. But it was meeting the great Dr. John Hunter that finally made me decide my vocation was for curing men's bodies rather than their souls."

Georgy wrinkled her brow in an effort of memory. "I have heard people speak of Dr. Hunter," she said, slowly. "He died when I was only a schoolgirl, I think — "

"Seven years ago, in 1793," supplied Graham. "That was the year I met him. It was my first year up at Oxford, and I'd come to London on a spree with some other students during the vac. One of us became involved in a brawl — you know how these things go, I dare say, as you have brothers — and his arm got broken. I used what small knowledge I'd picked up from my uncle to render some primitive help until they could get a doctor. It happened quite close to St. George's Hospital, and they managed to get hold of the great man himself."

"What happened then?" prompted Georgy, as he paused.

"Oh, he took a look at the injury, said it was a simple fracture, and would do well enough with the improvised splint I had used. Then he asked who'd done the setting. I was a bit hang-dog about admitting to it, as you may well imagine, but he just nodded, and stared at me, seeming to size me up. He asked if I was studying medicine at the University. When I said I wasn't, he seemed put out. "Then you ought to be, young man," he said. "I don't know what you're trying to do, but this is what you're cut out for. Get your degree in medicine, and afterwards I'll take you on as a pupil in surgery." And all at once I knew he was right, and this was what I'd wanted to do all along. My one regret is that I never had the chance to study under him, for he died a few months afterwards."

"Did your father raise no objection to the change of plan?"

He shrugged. "My father's too wise a man to oppose a natural inclination of such serious import. A reluctant clergyman is no good either to God or man."

"I suppose so," replied Georgy, slowly. "If a man has of necessity to earn a livelihood, then obviously he will do better at something for which he has natural talents. It's not a subject to which I've given much thought — " She hesitated, not liking to add the words that were in her mind.

He was able to supply them himself. "Of course not. I dare say few of your acquaintance are at the necessity of earning a living."

She stole a look at him. His tone was matter-of-fact, but was there just a shade of embarrassment in the expressive dark eyes? Suddenly she was conscious of a desire to put him at his ease.

"It might be better for some of them — notably my brothers — if they were," she said, emphatically. "Hugh, of course, has an estate to manage; but George and Freddy so far have nothing of any significance to do with their time. That's no doubt why they get up to such wild starts every now and then. Come to think of it," she acknowledged, with a sudden flash of self-realization, "I do myself, and possibly for the same reason. But there's no remedy, in my case. There is nothing of importance for women to do in the world."

"Except to marry and have children," he replied. "And what can be more important than that, pray?"

She grimaced. "It's a talent every maidservant possesses — every animal, come to that. Is our work in the world to be no more significant than that of the beasts in the field?"

He looked at her in astonishment. "Surely you can't truly think that, Miss Eversley? I have always believed that women considered motherhood their highest destiny and their supreme achievement."

"Oh, yes, I know!" Her tone was impatient, but he felt that her irritation was more for herself than for him. "And so it is — in a way. But that's only one side of our natures. There is another side." She paused, struggling to express thoughts that she could herself only partly apprehend. "You believe — most men believe — that women are frivolous creatures, their minds filled with every kind of triviality, and totally closed to reason. But we are as rational as you, Dr. Graham, and as well fitted to do work of importance in the world, if only men would see fit to trust us to do it. But what happens? We are not even allowed to equip ourselves with a rational education, but must spend weary hours learning to wield a needle when perhaps we have more talent with a pen, or to make ourselves agreeable in a drawing-room, when we are longing to drive a curricle and pair headlong, or share in some other sport which is only allowed to our brothers! I ask you, is it fair, sir?"

"You make out a very good case," he said, with a smile. "But yours is an exceptional nature — I imagine few females feel as you do on this subject."

"More than you might suppose," she retorted. "I'm for ever meeting them, and they are by no means always young women, either! There was quite an elderly lady — a Mrs. Lybbe Powys — staying with some friends of ours only recently, and she gave vent to similar opinions one afternoon when all the women of the party were left together for a few hours. And you may depend on it that there are many more who have such feelings without ever expressing them, or even allowing themselves to acknowledge their existence!"

"You may be right. All the same, I don't quite see what is to be done about it," he said, easily.

"Oh, if that isn't just like a man!" exclaimed Georgy impatiently. "You acknowledge an injustice, but refuse to take any action to set it right!"

He looked down into the flashing green eyes that were turned up to his, and some of his habitual calm left him.

"If any action of mine could serve to gratify your wishes, you might count on me," he said, spontaneously.

"Oh!" She was momentarily taken aback. "Do you mean it?"

"Yes, I mean it." He returned his gaze

to the road, speaking in level tones in spite of the erratic behaviour of his pulse. "But I fear my goodwill won't be of much avail in this case — you need to convert the world at large — particularly your own world, the world of fashion."

"Pooh, I don't care that much for the *ton*!" she said, snapping her fingers.

The gesture jarred her wounded arm, and drew a wince from her. He pulled up at once and turned solicitously towards her.

"You've hurt yourself — you must take more care," he insisted, lifting her arm and inspecting his handiwork. After a moment, satisfied that the bandage was firm, he placed the arm so that it lay resting across her knees. "Perhaps I should have put your arm in a sling, so that you wouldn't be tempted to incautious movements," he said, in a deliberately light tone.

"Certainly caution is never my strongest point," she admitted, with a twinkle in her eyes. "I fear I am a sad case, and quite beyond your doctoring, sir!"

He was still leaning towards her looking down into her face, his fingers resting lightly on the bare arm from which the sleeve had been cut away. For a moment he felt all the magnetism of her dancing green eyes, and knew a swift, strong urge to gather her up into his arms.

"You are beyond me in every way," he said, hoarsely, scarcely knowing what words he uttered.

She made a little incoherent sound, and seemed to sway towards him. His head felt light, as though he had drunk too much wine.

The spell was broken abruptly by the sound of horses trotting rapidly down the road. The next moment, voices were calling Georgiana by name.

Graham drew away from her just as the riders reached the gig, and reined in beside it.

"So here you are!" drawled Pamyngton, sweeping his hat from his head. "Servant, Graham! A fine morning."

The other rider was Curshawe, and he treated the matter less calmly.

"Wherever have you been, Miss Georgiana?" he asked. "When you did not appear for breakfast, Mrs. Eversley became alarmed and asked us to ride out and see if we could find you." His glance, which had been ranging jealously over both occupants of the gig, now lighted on her bare arm and the bandage encircling it. He gave a horrified start. "Good God! You are injured! Whatever has happened?"

Pamyngton echoed the query, though in a more restrained manner. Graham gave a short, lucid account of Georgy's rescue of the child.

"It was madness!" exclaimed Curshawe, at the end of the recital. "You should never have ventured it, Miss Georgy! You might have been killed!"

"The child almost certainly would have been, but for Miss Eversley's brave action," remarked Graham, in a dry tone.

"How bad is the injury?" asked Pamyngton.

"Nothing serious," replied Graham. "A week should see it healed completely, and it will leave no permanent scar."

"All the same," expostulated Curshawe, "Miss Eversley should not be jolted back to Fulmer Towers in this style. I wonder you did not send to the house for a carriage, Dr. Graham."

"Oh, have done, Mr. Curshawe!" exclaimed Georgy, in an impatient tone. "Dr. Graham would have sent for a carriage, but I didn't wish it, as I feared the message might alarm Susan. I am perfectly all right, thanks to the good offices of the doctor and Mrs. and Miss Hume, and I wish to hear no more on the subject! Of all things, I dislike a fuss!"

Curshawe coloured up, apologized, and said no more. Graham took up the reins, and the gig proceeded on its way to Fulmer Towers, closely accompanied by the two riders.

10

Freddy Talks

DURING the week that followed, Georgiana had no need to seek out Graham, for the doctor called at Fulmer Towers every day to enquire after the health of both his patients.

Georgiana's arm mended quickly, and she soon found herself longing to return to her normal pastimes and amusements. Everyone in the house seemed determined to take her injury more seriously than she herself did, however. Four days after the accident, when she announced at breakfast her intention of going riding for a spell, it caused quite a storm of protest from the others.

"Do you think that's quite wise, my love?" asked Susan, mildly, when the first outcry had died down a little.

"Of course not — she must have run mad!" exclaimed Aunt Lavinia.

Everyone agreed with this view, except Freddy and George, who both returned to their newspapers, knowing the folly of opposing Georgy too strongly. No doubt Hugh, who was not present in the room at the moment, would eventually put a stop to her scheme. Curshawe spoke at greater length than anyone else in his efforts to persuade Miss Georgy not to contemplate such a step.

"Why not?" demanded Georgy, impatient of their fuss.

"If I am fit to dance at a ball tomorrow, I can very well go riding today, as far as I can see!"

"Dear lady, it is not at all the same thing!" protested Curshawe, ignoring a signal from both George and Freddy to hold his peace. They sighed, knowing too well that opposition only served to strengthen their rebellious sister's determination. "Ask the doctor, I beg of you, when he calls. I am confident that he will not permit it."

"Dr. Graham may give what *advice* he chooses," replied Georgiana, tartly. "As to *permission*, I seek that from no one. I am my own mistress. Besides," she went on, in a slightly mollified tone, "he makes no to-do about my injury, which he says — quite truthfully — is nothing but a scratch. Susan made me ask him the other day if it would hinder me from dancing as otherwise she was going to postpone the ball; and he said there could be no reason why I should not do anything I myself felt equal to. That is all the guidance I need — or want."

Pamyngton had remained silent after his original involuntary protest, which had been swallowed up in the more vociferous ones of his companions. He now raised his head, hearing sounds from the hall.

"I think that is Graham now," he remarked, looking at Georgiana.

Her hands went involuntarily to her hair, smoothing an errant curl. Both she and Susan rose from the table just as the footman came in to announce that Dr. Graham was awaiting his patients in the morning-room.

He saw Susan first, attended by the elderly family nurse who had principal charge of little Maria, and who was to assist Dr. Hume when the time came for the confinement. Mrs. Eversley was now in the last month of her pregnancy, and Graham had promised his uncle to call on her frequently just to be sure that all was going well.

"I need scarcely remind you, John," Dr. Hume had said, before leaving for Scotland, "that the Honourable Hugh Eversley's wife is a most important client of mine — apart from the fact that she's a gey sweet young woman, and for her own sake, I want nothing to go wrong. Not that I think it will, mind; but it would be just as well to keep a close eye on her while I'm away."

Lately, reflected Graham, he had more than fulfilled the promise. Would he have called so often at Fulmer Towers, he wondered, if the fascinating Miss Eversley had not been staying there with her brother? He shied away from the question, telling himself that Georgiana Eversley was at present his patient.

All the same his hands were not quite steady as he changed the dressing on her arm. Mrs. Ledibond, the nurse, noticed this with some misgiving as she gently eased up Georgy's sleeve to reveal the bandage. She need not have worried, however. As soon as Graham had removed the bandage, all personal feelings were forgotten as he inspected the wound with professional interest.

"Capital!" he exclaimed, in a satisfied tone. "You've a good healing skin, ma'am, for this is knitting together splendidly. You feel no pain from it now?"

Georgiana shook her head, turning the full power of her green eyes upon him. "Not a bit of it! Pray, when can I dispense with this clumsy bandage?"

He hurriedly lowered his glance to her arm again. "Not just yet," he said, a shade curtly. "Though a much lighter bandage will serve you now. We'll see how it goes on in another few days."

"She is talking of riding today," put in Susan, who was sitting in the same room in a wing chair with two cushions at her back. "Pray tell her how foolish it is, Dr. Graham! We have all tried to dissuade her, but to no purpose."

"Of all things, I detest a fuss!" remarked Georgy. "You should know that, Sue. Well, now you have heard for yourself what Dr. Graham says, perhaps you'll allow me to go my own way."

"I said nothing about your riding a horse today, however," pointed out Dr. Graham, calmly, as he began to place a fresh bandage on her arm.

He looked up in time to catch the now familiar flash in her green eyes.

"Did you not?" she asked, loftily. "Well, it's no matter. You said it's healing nicely — and, anyway, I intend to go."

Graham made no reply, but finished tying the bandage, then stood a little away from her while Mrs. Ledibond arranged Georgy's sleeve over it.

"Not today, Miss Eversley," he said, in a pleasant though firm tone, "perhaps in another day or two, when we dispense altogether with a bandage."

She set her mouth mutinously. "I want to go now — today! I am sick to death of being mewed up in this house!"

He raised dark eyebrows. "Surely there's someone who might take you out for a drive? I don't recommend a jolting carriage for Mrs. Eversley" — he glanced at Susan — "but it's quite different for you."

"But I don't want to ride tamely abroad in a carriage!" exclaimed Georgy, petulantly. "It's not near such sport as riding on horseback!"

"Doesn't that rather depend on who's driving, ma'am?"

Graham's irrepressible sense of humour brought the words to his lips before he could suppress them. He tried to soften them with one of his crooked smiles.

"Oh!" stormed Georgy, stamping her foot. "You are — I detest you!"

Mrs. Ledibond, who had nursed Georgy, too, as a child, clucked her tongue reprovingly. "Now, come, Miss Georgy!" she expostulated, forgetting for a moment the years between; "That's no way to speak to the doctor!"

"On the contrary, Nurse," said Graham, laughing, "I richly deserved it. Miss Eversley, let's make a bargain. If I promise never again to refer to your skill as a whip, will you in your turn undertake to leave your horse riding till another day?"

"I'll promise you nothing!" The auburn

curls tossed angrily.

"Ungracious," commented Graham, coolly. "Well, ma'am, I did my best to resolve our difference by fair means, now I must resort to other measures."

"What other measures?" echoed Georgy, suspiciously. "Anyway, that will be more in keeping with your nature!"

A choking sound from Susan claimed their attention. She was sitting in her chair doubled up with helpless laughter. "Oh — you're so droll, you two!" she gurgled, while tears of mirth came to her eyes. "You go on — as if — as if — you had known each other all your lives — instead of — of — " She stopped, and let out a crowing sound — "Any two people less like — like doctor and patient — I never did see!"

"Pray stop her, sir!" begged nurse, running to Susan's side. "Mrs. Eversley, ma'am — my pet — you mustn't take on so — 'twill do you no good! Pray calm yourself!"

She began to pat Susan's hands. Graham left Georgiana abruptly, and came to Susan's side.

"She'll take no harm," he said,

reassuringly. "All the same, ma'am, it may moderate your mirth when I ask you to forbid Miss Eversley to take a horse out today."

He was quite right. Susan stopped laughing immediately. "Me?" she gasped. "You can't suppose, sir, that Georgy will heed me any more than she does you!"

"Then I see I must apply to your husband," replied Graham, quietly. "Perhaps you'll be good enough to send someone to ask if he will spare me a moment?"

Georgiana's face fell for a moment; but she quickly recovered, turning a hostile look on Graham.

"Very well," she said, coldly. "You win — this hand. There will be others, never fear — and you may not come off so well next time."

He flashed a crooked smile, and gave her a curt little bow.

"I fear it's a risk I must take, ma'am."

★ ★ ★

Viscount Pamyngton was, as Hugh had once remarked, not the man to wear his heart on his sleeve; but he had his full share of perception and certainly had not failed to notice the tense atmosphere surrounding Dr. Graham and Georgiana at the moment when Curshawe and himself had met them in the road after Georgy's accident. He was quite used to seeing men's heads turned by the lovely, unpredictable Miss Eversley. He had come to accept it as a commonplace during the last few London seasons, since he had himself joined her court. Judging by what had gone before, he would not have supposed that the doctor was at all likely to fall under Georgy's spell; but no man could be safe where a girl had so much beauty, charm and that indefinable extra something which set her apart from other females. Pamyngton saw no cause for wonder, and even less for alarm, if Graham was on the brink of falling in love with Georgy.

What did cause him some private speculation was the element of interest which his quick senses perceived on the lady's side. For the first time since he had known her, Georgiana Eversley seemed to be going out of her way deliberately to entrap a man; and a man, at that, with whom she was unlikely to have any thought of marriage. It was all very puzzling, and the puzzle grew during the days that followed.

The doctor called every day; and Pamyngton noticed the care with which Georgiana dressed for these visits, and the pains she was at to prolong them beyond their strictly necessary professional duration. Moreover, whenever George suggested that his friend Jock Graham should join their party for any social occasion, it was not difficult for a close observer to see how welcome the suggestion was to Georgiana. Could it be, Pamyngton asked himself doubtfully, that the Incomparable had taken a tumble herself at last? In spite of his observations, he could not believe this. There was too much evidence of calculation rather than emotion in her actions. He shrugged his shoulders, and wished he knew what her game was. Perhaps he would have done better to refuse Beau Eversley's invitation to Fulmer Towers, after all. He had hoped that a few weeks in the comparative seclusion of the country might bring himself and Georgy closer than was possible in the constant whirl of social engagements and admirers which made up her life in Town. He had realized that he would have another of her admirers to contend with in Buckinghamshire, but the thought of Henry Curshawe as a rival had brought no alarm to his mind. It should be easy enough to outwit that dull dog Curshawe. In the event, it had not been so easy. He had underestimated the tenacity of purpose, the sheer nuisance value of the other man. There had been fewer opportunities at Fulmer Towers than he had hoped of a tête-à-tête with Georgy; but even those few had always been ruined by Curshawe, who persisted in shadowing his rival to a degree that was ludicrous. If the man did not stop dogging his footsteps soon, thought Pamyngton in exasperation, something would have to be done; though what he could not imagine.

His disgust with Curshawe reached its peak on the day when Georgy wanted to go riding. She came flouncing into the parlour after her interview with Graham, and closed the door with a decided snap.

Only Curshawe, Pamyngton and her two brothers remained in the room reading. They all looked up for a moment from their newspapers as she entered.

"You look in a bit of a pet," remarked Freddy with a twinkle. "I collect your friend Graham didn't support your scheme of going riding?"

"He's no friend of mine!" snapped Georgy.

Freddy raised his brows. "Pity," he said, significantly. "You're not doing too well, are you, my dear, with not much more than a fortnight to go?"

Everyone's curiosity was aroused by this speech. George demanded what the devil Freddy meant, but received no answer. Georgy herself, when appealed to, answered hurriedly that it was just some of Freddy's nonsense. This satisfied George, but not either Pamyngton or Curshawe. The former had too much sense to labour the point, but Curshawe was not so wise.

"If it's nonsense, Miss Georgiana, may we not be privileged to share the jest? Not much more than a fortnight to go — to what, I wonder?"

He asked the question in an arch manner that set everyone's teeth on edge. George rose, tossed his newspaper aside, and made for the door.

"Whatever it is, we're all likely to be back in Town by then," he said. "Well, if Jock's finished his business here for today, I'll go and have a chat with him."

"Can Frederick mean that your injury is not mending as it should?" persisted Curshawe, with an anxious look. "That it will scarcely be recovered by the time you return to your own home? Dear lady, should you not perhaps take a second opinion on it? I've no doubt that this medico friend of your brother's is an excellent man in his way; but, after all, he is very young, and cannot have had a great deal of experience. I am persuaded that you should get a man from London — someone older, more used to dealing with things of this nature. My mother would willingly recommend you to our own family doctor, who brought us all successfully through a number of ailments — "

"More's the pity," murmured Freddy,

160

in an aside, which Pamyngton just managed to catch, and which set his lips twitching.

" . . . and has been in practice for at least thirty years," went on Curshawe's voice, inexorably. "Shall I find her now, and ask her to write to him on your behalf? I know she will be only too happy to serve you in this, as in any other way she can."

He started towards the door as he finished.

"No, pray do not!" exclaimed Georgy, sharply.

He halted for a moment. "I know how you dislike a fuss, ma'am, and believe me, I consider it does you great credit. But when it is a matter of one's health, you know, it is better to make a little fuss than to risk overlooking something which could be serious later on. I well remember my mother saying — "

"Oh, for God's sake!" exclaimed Freddy, throwing down his newspaper and jumping to his feet. "Have done, Curshawe! This is nothing to do with Georgy's health, man, but a matter of a wager we have together! And I must say it don't look as if she's got an earthly hope of winning."

"A — a wager? Between Miss Georgy and yourself? But surely the fair sex do not indulge in such pastimes?" asked Curshawe, doubtfully.

"Don't they just!" answered Freddy, derisively. "I tell you what, Curshawe, you've led too sheltered a life by half! If you think my sister Georgy's one of these miss-ish girls, you're a long way out. No, the thing is, after she had that dust-up with Jock Graham — when she nearly ran him down, you know — I bet her that she couldn't make him — "

"Freddy, no!" exploded Georgy, launching herself towards him. "Don't you dare!"

He shook her off, laughing. "Why not? Where's the harm? I'm sure they'll find it as rich a joke as I do — though they must keep it to themselves. The thing is," he went on with his explanation, "to win our wager, Georgy's got to work on Jock so that he makes her a declaration before either party leaves the district. And as there's something less than three weeks to go, and they're still at daggers drawn,

162

I think I can safely count on a win. Well, what d'ye say? Ain't it rich? Don't know when I ever came across a couple who detest each other so thoroughly. A fine pair of lovebirds they'd make!" He went off into a series of deepthroated chuckles.

Curshawe eyed him severely. "I'm sorry to tell you, Frederick, that I find your levity misplaced," he said, heavily. "What's more, I am quite sure that your sister could never be a party to anything so — " he paused, seeking for the right words "of such a nature. I'm sure that, were either of your elder brothers to learn that you had made such an improper bet — "

"You don't mean that you'd actually peach on us to Hugh or George?" asked Freddy, indignantly. "Well, if that don't beat old Boney himself! I thought you were a bit of a queer fish, Curshawe, but I never — "

During these interchanges, Pamyngton had remained silent. The story of the wager threw new light on all that had puzzled him of late in Georgiana's behaviour. His chief emotion now was one of relief.

"I don't think you need worry," he said, interrupting Freddy before that young man should say something too uncivil to Curshawe. "Neither of us will mention this matter to anyone else — eh, Curshawe?"

He directed a long, steady look at his rival, and then glanced at Georgy, who stood with clenched hands and flushed cheeks at her brother's side.

"Thank you, my lord, but I believe I can answer for myself," replied Curshawe, with dignity. "Naturally, I would hesitate to say anything which might embarrass Miss Georgiana in any way. And as I am certain that she can have no part in her brother's jest — which I consider to be in doubtful taste, though I am sorry to say so — then I shall be glad to forget that I ever heard anything about such a wager."

Suddenly Georgy stamped her foot. "Oh!" she exclaimed, fighting back the tears as she rushed from the room, "I detest you all — you are stupid beyond belief!"

11

Two's Company

GEORGIANA rushed straight up to her bedchamber. Outside the door, she almost collided with Susan, who was coming away from her own room. She apologized hastily and flung open the door; but Susan had seen the expression on her face, and followed her into the room.

"What's amiss, love?" she asked, closing the door.

"Oh, nothing!" Georgy flung herself down on the bed and began to pound the mattress with her fists. "Only that I am sick to death of the country, and of everyone in this house — or nearly everyone!"

Susan sat down beside her. "Is it Dr. Graham who's upset you so by saying you must not ride?"

"Not only that — everyone else is just as stupid and boring! I declare,"

165

exploded Georgy, tears giving way to anger as she turned a fierce expression towards her sister-in-law, "if that prosy creature Henry Curshawe treats me to any more of his moralizing, I shall do him a mischief! As for Freddy — he's the greatest beast in nature! I shall never forgive him — it's all his fault!"

"What's all his fault, dearest?"

"Oh, never mind! Only he must go and blab things out, like the ninny hammer he is! And then that stupid little man Curshawe takes it all so seriously, while even Pam — "

She broke off, and ran distracted fingers through her tumbled hair.

"What about Lord Pamyngton?" prompted Susan gently.

"Oh, nothing — only I thought he had a sense of humour, that's all! I see I was wrong."

"My love, I haven't the faintest notion what you are talking of," said Susan, in a bewildered tone. "Can't you tell me the whole? Come, we always used to confide in each other, and it never failed to make us feel better, now, did it? Tell me everything, from the beginning — do!"

Georgy hesitated, then shook her head. "This is different, Sue. For one thing, you might be shocked. For another, I can't risk it coming to Hugh's ears, for I know he most certainly wouldn't approve."

"Hugh disapprove! Georgy, whatever can you have done?"

Too late, Georgy saw that she had alarmed her sister-in-law.

"Oh, it's nothing to look like that about!" she said hastily. "It's only some stupid bet I made with Freddy, and he has no more sense than to blurt it all out in front of Pam and Mr. Curshawe."

"Oh, is that all?" asked Susan relieved. "What was the subject of the wager — or mayn't I ask?"

Georgy shook her head. Susan looked doubtful again.

"As long as you didn't undertake to do anything dangerous," she demurred.

To her surprise, Georgy laughed.

"Not in the least dangerous."

"Oh, well, that's all right then. But why," asked Susan, as the thought suddenly struck her, "were Lord Pamyngton and Mr. Curshawe shocked at your entering into a wager with your own brother? Surely even a veritable stickler for the proprieties couldn't object to that? And — yes, Georgy! You're keeping something back, I know! — why should you be so convinced that Hugh would disapprove, and that even I might, too?" She took Georgy's arm, and looked at her coaxingly. "What is this wager? Come, I think you'd better tell me?"

Georgy shook her head, and rose from the bed. "No, not now. I will tell you at some time, never fear, but not just at present. No, it's no use to argue or cajole, Sue" — as her sister-in-law began to protest — "my mind is quite made up. Let's change the subject. What shall I wear at the ball tomorrow?"

Beau Eversley had at first been a little doubtful about his wife's scheme — largely inspired by Georgy — to give an informal ball for their guests and the neighbouring gentry. He feared that the excitement might be unwise in her present condition. But Susan had insisted that something of the kind was due to their guests, and that she could enjoy watching others dance almost as much as taking part herself. Eventually he agreed on condition that numbers should be kept down, and that Susan should retire early from the festivities, leaving Georgy to play the part of hostess. Invitations had accordingly been sent out to a score or so of their neighbours. There had, of course, been an invitation for Georgy's friend, Dr. Graham; and his cousin Miss Anne Hume had been included since Georgy's accident.

Seeing that she was not likely to persuade Georgy to tell her anything more at present, Susan allowed the subject to be changed. After a short session spent in pulling out gowns and debating their rival merits or demerits, Susan went away to write some letters, and Georgy tidied her tumbled hair and left her room.

She found Pamyngton standing at the foot of the staircase as she descended it. She was still out of humour, and would have passed him without speaking, but he gently detained her.

"I know it's not at all the same thing," he said, with a disarming smile, "but I wondered if perhaps a spin in my curricle might help to console you for your lost ride?"

She looked for a moment as though she would refuse. Then she nodded. "Oh, I may as well."

He bowed, and began to turn away to issue the necessary order for the curricle to be brought round from the stables. Something in his quiet manner made her relent.

"I'm sorry, Pam," she said, impetuously. "That was uncommon rude of me, just because I felt cross. You are always so kind and forbearing and there are times when I don't deserve it. I'll fetch my bonnet and pelisse, and we'll go directly."

"No hurry," he said. "I'll await you in the parlour."

She turned to run upstairs. The door of the parlour opened, and Henry Curshawe came out. He exclaimed in satisfaction on seeing Georgy.

"Ah, Miss Georgy, I'm so pleased to have found you! Will you do me the honour to come for a drive with me? Your brother George has very kindly offered me the use of his curricle."

"Thank you, Mr. Curshawe, but I have already accepted a similar offer from Pam," Georgy replied, with her usual good humour. "Perhaps some other time."

She continued on her way upstairs, and Pamyngton turned towards the parlour.

"You timed your invitation well," Curshawe flung after him.

Pamyngton turned. "A great deal depends upon good timing, I find."

He could not help a certain feeling of satisfaction in having managed to outwit Curshawe at last. It was to be short-lived. He had barely started along the road with Georgiana, now completely restored in spirits, sitting up beside him looking entrancing in a deep blue pelisse trimmed with white fur, when they heard the sound of following hoofs. A moment later, a horseman drew level with them, and they saw to their chagrin that it was Curshawe.

"I thought I'd ride with you," he said, with the air of one conferring a favour. "You'll only be jaunting along, I imagine, so we can go side by side."

"Not much room for that on these roads," replied Pamyngton coolly.

"Oh, I don't know. There's very little traffic at present, and I can easily drop back if I see anything coming."

There was nothing to be done but to suffer his presence with as good a grace as possible, and for some miles they travelled along side by side. Conversation was desultory. Curshawe's presence inhibited the easy badinage which usually took place between Georgiana and Pamyngton, and he himself had nothing to contribute that his companions found either interesting or stimulating. Moreover, he could not always hear what passed between the two in the curricle; and he kept on demanding to be told what they had said, in a way which both found an irritation.

At length, Georgy showed signs of impatience with the whole business. "Let them go, Pam!" she urged. "I'm tired of dawdling along in this tame manner! It was not for this that I accepted your offer of a drive!"

"Do you think I should?" he asked, looking down at her with a quizzical expression. "Curshawe may take it amiss, you know."

"What's that you say, Pamyngton?" queried Curshawe, sharply. "Did I hear you mention my name?"

"Oh, for goodness sake!" exclaimed Georgy, sotto voce. "I tell you, Pam, if you think more of offending him than of pleasing me, I have done with you!"

Pamyngton grimaced, and leaned sideways to address the other man. "Nothing will do for Miss Georgy but that I should gallop my horses. Do you mind dropping back?"

Curshawe's face clouded, and he muttered something which Pamyngton could not quite catch, but he drew away from the curricle, even if reluctantly.

Pamyngton straightened up in his seat, flung Georgy a mocking glance, and settled his hat more firmly on his head.

"Hold tight, then!"

He dropped his hands, and the horses leapt forward.

Georgy's heart lifted with exhilaration. This was living to the full, she thought, this swift movement that sent her blood coursing through her body, bringing the colour to her cheeks and making her eyes sparkle.

"Faster!" she urged. "Faster!"

And Pamyngton, briefly looking into that animated face, obeyed. The curricle sped like an arrow along the narrow white road, leaving Curshawe a very small blob in the distance.

"This is prodigious!" breathed Georgy. "It's — oh! — better than anything I can think of!"

He smiled and shook his head at her, reining in his horses only slightly as they came to a bend in the road. When they had rounded the bend, he was about to give the animals their heads again; but he checked on seeing a stationary vehicle a little farther along on the other side of the road.

"Afraid we'll have to pass this at a more sedate pace," he warned her, indicating the vehicle with his whip.

She pouted in protest. "What a shame! Never mind — afterwards, we shall go even faster! What do you say, Pam?"

"It shall be as you wish." He sounded amused. "But you are certainly an intrepid young lady — as Freddy once said, a devil to go."

They were now close to the stationary vehicle, which was a gig. The driver of it seemed to be much occupied with his passenger, a young lady in a becoming pink bonnet, for he was leaning close to her and gazing earnestly into her eyes.

"A pair of lovebirds, seemingly," murmured Pamyngton.

Georgy glanced at the occupants of the gig, then gave a start. They were none other than Dr. Graham and his cousin Anne Hume.

As the curricle drew close beside the gig to pass, Graham turned away from his cousin, stowed away a handkerchief which he was holding, and immediately recognized Georgiana and Pamyngton.

He bowed and greeted them. Pamyngton returned the greeting, and courteously asked Miss Hume how she did.

"Very well, I thank you," she replied, shyly. "That is to say, I did have some grit in my eye just now, but John has this minute removed it for me."

Pamyngton gravely remarked that this was fortunate. "We shall look forward to seeing you both tomorrow," he concluded, "at Mrs. Eversley's ball."

There were smiles and bows on both sides, and the curricle drew past, continuing on its way.

Georgy looked back, and saw that the gig was also moving off; at the same moment Curshawe, riding hard, appeared round the bend.

"Well?" asked Pamyngton. "Shall I let them go again, before he catches up with us?"

Georgy shook her head. Her face was withdrawn. "No, not now. I am no longer in the mood for it. Pray take me home, Pam."

12

The Eavesdropper

JOHN GRAHAM hired a carriage from the local inn for the evening of the ball. He might be careless enough of his own consequence to arrive at Fulmer Towers in a gig, but he recognized that this would not do for his cousin.

"I only hope the thing will hold together until we get there," he said doubtfully as he handed her into it. "Damned if I ever saw such a ramshackle vehicle!"

Anne seated herself on the faded upholstery with a happy little smile on her face. "I think it's splendid, Cousin John, really I do!"

He looked her over appraisingly. "It's nothing like grand enough to match your finery tonight, Anne. That pink gown becomes you — and what on earth have you done to your hair?"

"Don't you like it?" she asked, anxiously,

carefully giving a pat to the elaborate Grecian coiffure which she had managed to achieve with the aid of her mother. "It — it doesn't look absurd, does it? Mama said it does — but then she is a trifle old-fashioned in her views on dress — "

"No such thing," he replied, with another searching glance. "On the contrary, it makes you look all the crack — but not nearly so much like yourself, if you know what I mean."

Anne did know what he meant, and her eyes shone. She had spent a great deal of time and most of her allowance in an endeavour to look different, to appear more exciting and interesting than usual. From his reply, she judged she had succeeded.

Her complacency was short-lived, however. When they arrived at Fulmer Towers, her first sight of Georgiana Eversley removed it immediately. Georgy was wearing a sea-green dress that flowed softly over her perfect figure; and that magnificent tawny hair of hers, thought Anne ruefully, glowing in the light of the chandeliers, could scarcely fail to draw every eye. She noticed with misgiving that it certainly did not fail to claim her cousin's attention.

Although he greeted Georgiana briefly enough, passing on to chat for a while to her brother George, Anne saw that his eyes lingered on Miss Eversley whenever she chanced to come within his range of vision. Anne experienced the same sinking of spirits that she had felt once before, and almost decided that her evening was ruined.

As soon as the dancing began, she took a livelier view of matters. Her cousin partnered her not only for the first dance, which she had expected, but also for the second, which she had not. He was at his most gay and amusing, laughing at her fears that she might not get the steps right, and whirling her round with a careless grace that tugged at her heart. She tried to tell herself severely that she must not think tenderly of him. He had given absolutely no sign of thinking of her in any other than a cousinly way. But her heart, now as light as her feet, refused to heed this sober counsel. Her grave brown eyes shone as she laughed in response to his light-hearted chatter. Pamyngton, who was partnering Georgy, glanced with an indulgent smile at the cousins, as they passed close to them.

"Your doctor's cousin is a pretty little creature," he remarked. "All brown and wholesome, like a sweet nut."

"Lud, Pam, you're lyrical, all of a sudden!" scoffed Georgy. Her eyes rested thoughtfully on the pair, and the faintest of frowns creased her forehead. "Yes, she is pretty — she has changed her hair style, and it gives her a more arresting look."

"They appear very well pleased with each other," continued Pam, as they moved on. "How do you feel now about the likehood of winning your wager with Freddy?"

"Pray don't mention that stupid wager again!" said Georgy, with a snap. "Freddy had no business to tell you of it — and, anyway, it was all a joke!"

"To hear is to obey," replied Pamyngton, smiling. "Only please don't scowl at me so fiercely. It makes me lose my steps."

She laughed. "As if anything could! But I beg your pardon — you must think me a sad wretch!"

"Must I?" he answered, in a different tone. "You're quite wrong. Some day perhaps I may tell you what I really do think — but this is neither the time nor the place."

She glanced briefly up at him. For a fleeting moment the expression in his eyes was unguarded. She looked away again quickly, with a slightly flustered air.

When the dance came to an end, Freddy Eversley claimed Anne's hand for the next. She acquiesced with a shy little smile, though she would far rather have danced with her cousin all evening, had this been possible. But such a breach of good manners was not to be thought of, even if John himself had shown any sign of wishing for it. Instead, he readily yielded her hand to the newcomer, and turned away to seek a fresh partner for himself.

He looked across the room to where Georgiana was standing amidst a small group of people, and he took a few steps in that direction. Then he halted, uncertain whether to continue. As he stood hesitating, Georgiana chanced to turn round, and their eyes met. The intervening space was crowded, but for the few moments that they shared this glance, it seemed to John Graham that there was no one else in the room but the two of them. It was an experience that he could never forget for the rest of his life.

He caught his breath, like someone who has just plunged into ice-cold water. Then he moved slowly towards her, as though dazed.

Afterwards, he could never remember the exact words he used to ask her for the next dance, although he could recall her answer quite clearly.

"I am sorry, but I'm already promised for this dance."

The simple words seemed to him to be charged with a special meaning. Or was it just that in this one moment of time he was living on a plane of higher sensitivity? For once in his experience, he felt out of his depth.

"You can't be!" He answered her without thinking. "That's to say — I won't let you be!"

Her lovely green eyes widened. "But I *am*. Mr. Curshawe claimed this dance some time ago. I'm sorry — I'm afraid there's nothing to be done — perhaps later on — "

She broke off in confusion, as he still stood there silently regarding her as though he had never seen her before. A little colour came into her cheeks. She saw one or two people looking at them covertly, and she began to lose some of her poise. In another moment, she might have said something more; but Curshawe presented himself to lead her into the dance. She gave Graham one small, timid smile, and then she was gone.

He remained standing where he was until he suddenly realized that everyone else had moved from the spot, and he was conspicuously alone. A surge of alien emotions troubled him. He needed real solitude to master them, and cast about in his mind for somewhere he could go to be away from the crowd for a space. As the first chords of music struck up, he made his way to a conservatory which ran along one side of the house and which could be entered by a door leading off the ballroom.

The conservatory was quiet and dark. All kinds of exotic trees and shrubs grew here, and a few rustic benches were set well back in their shade, against the wall. The only faint light came from small coloured lanterns which had been hung here and there more for effect than for illumination. He flung himself down on the first seat he came to; it was quite close to the door leading into the ballroom, but well screened from the view of anyone else who should chance to come that way. He had closed the door after him, and for the present he could be quite alone.

He needed to think. What had happened to him? He had shared a glance with a girl across a room full of other people, and instantly some mysterious element had entered his life. It was nonsense, of course. Although he had never experienced anything of the kind before, his medical mind, he told himself, could recognize it for what it was. It was no more than Nature up to her old tricks. Why, he did not even like or approve of

Miss Eversley! She was spoilt, arrogant and selfish. In spite of himself, his mouth softened. She was also brave, frank and as disarming as a winsome child. But no matter for that, he thought sternly, this nonsense must stop at once. A man in his circumstances could not afford to nourish any tender feelings towards a female as much above his reach as she was. A society belle and a young doctor who, although well born, had yet his way to make in the world!

The notion was ludicrous — it would certainly appear so to her family. It was not even as if medicine happened to be a particularly respected profession. Only consider the Gloucestershire surgeon Dr. Jenner who had recently toiled all the way up to London from his country home in order to try and interest people in this new discovery of his, the vaccination against smallpox. He had finally left in disgust and humiliation, because no one there would believe in its efficacy. Yet there could be little doubt, from the evidence, that vaccination was the best method so far discovered to beat that dreadful scourge which killed and disfigured thousands. This is what it would always be like for the doctor, thought Graham; a constant fight against ignorance and the fear of what was new. A girl like Georgiana, he realized suddenly, was just the kind of female to make a splendid partner in that fight. She was pluck to the backbone. He gave an impatient movement. What nonsense was he thinking now? She was as remote from him as the stars which gleamed outside in the October sky.

The sound of the door opening and closing jerked him from his reverie; a moment later, he heard a low murmur of voices, and footsteps approaching. Evidently a couple had come here in search of privacy. Well, he would wait until they had gone past him, and then he would slip back into the ballroom, unobserved. It was time he was getting back, in any event.

But the newcomers did not pass; instead, they halted only a few paces away from where he was sitting, and directly in the way he would have to take to reach the door. He cursed his luck, then consoled himself with the thought

186

that they might continue walking in a few minutes, thus giving him a chance to escape. In the meantime, they could not see him; and although he could dimly make out two figures through the foliage, he could not see enough to recognize who they were. He shrank back into his seat with an impatient movement. The next moment, he jerked himself bolt upright as he recognized Georgiana's voice. He could hear every word quite clearly.

She spoke in an impatient tone. "I mustn't be long absent from the ballroom, so whatever you wish to say, sir, I beg you will be brief."

"I will do my best, but you cannot understand, Miss Georgiana — you don't know what torments I have endured!" answered her escort. In spite of its husky, emotional tone, Graham had no difficulty in identifying this voice as Curshawe's. "I can't keep silent any longer! It is too much to see that fellow Pamyngton always at your side."

"I have known Pam for a very long time," said Georgy, soothingly. "Pray don't be absurd, Mr. Curshawe!"

"There, you see — you call him by

a nickname, but I am always Mr. Curshawe! If only you could bring yourself to call me by my Christian name! Miss Georgy — you must allow me to tell you — "

It seemed to Graham, now feeling decidely uneasy, that Georgiana cut very quickly into Curshawe's speech, as though determined at all costs to avoid having to hear the end of it.

"But everyone calls Lord Pamyngton 'Pam'," she objected, quickly. "The nickname was given him in his schooldays, and has stuck to him ever since. And I have known you only a very short time, sir — it would not be at all proper for me to use your Christian name — I wonder you should think of such a thing! What would your mother say, do you suppose?"

"To tell you the truth, I don't care!" replied Curshawe, with a recklessness that was very different from his usual dry, measured style of speech. "I cannot bring myself to consider anyone's opinions or feelings except yours — and I think of yours all the time! I keep wondering what you really think of me, and whether I stand any chance at all with you — "

"Oh, *no!*" exclaimed Georgy, forcibly. "*Pray* don't say any more, Mr. Curshawe!"

Graham crouched in his corner with clenched fists and a ferocious expression on his face. The last thing he wanted was to eavesdrop on this abominable conversation, but what could he do, at this stage? To step out of his concealment now would only give acute embarrassment to all three of them. He ought to have made his presence known at once, but he had thought then that the couple would stroll past him, leaving him free to return to the ballroom unnoticed. He could not even make any attempt to move farther into the conservatory out of earshot because any movement on his part now would almost certainly lead to his discovery. The only possible course was to stay where he was, hoping that they would soon go, and meanwhile do his best not to listen. He made an honest attempt at this for a few minutes, but soon had to abandon it. The voices were too close at hand and the conversation of too much concern to him to be ignored.

"I must! I cannot keep silent any

longer! You must let me tell you how very much I admire you, Miss Georgiana, and that the dearest wish of my heart — "

"No!"

Agitatedly, she tried to stem the flow of words; but Curshawe was evidently well into his stride, thought Graham grimly, and brushed her exclamation heedlessly aside.

" . . . is to make you my wife. Oh, yes, I know that I should first have approached your father for permission to pay my addresses to you in form. But you will surely forgive my importunity, now that at last you know what a restraint I have been putting upon myself all these weeks! It is more than flesh and blood can bear! Miss Georgy, do not turn away from me! I beg of you, give me some answer — some hope!"

"I am honoured by your declaration, sir," said Georgy, in hurried, embarrassed tones, "but I did not wish you to make it — you must have seen that I tried to prevent you. And now we really must return to the ballroom, or our absence will be remarked."

"And is that all you have to say?" He sounded quite distracted. "Will you leave me without one word of hope? No, you cannot be so cruel, Miss Georgy, indeed you can't!"

Evidently at this point she was turning towards the door that led into the ballroom, and he must have tried to detain her.

"Kindly let me go," she said coldly. "I can say no more than I have done — it would be quite wrong in me to lead you on to hope for something that can never be."

"Why must it never be?" he demanded, in heated, jealous tones. "Is there someone else?"

"Really, Mr. Curshawe, you have no right to ask such a question! It is a great deal too bad of you to importune me in this way — and I don't propose to endure it for another moment. Be good enough to unhand me at once!"

"You don't need to answer me, for I know the answer already — "

"Release me at once, or I shall scream!"

At this juncture, Graham decided

reluctantly that he must intervene. He felt a certain amount of sympathy for Curshawe, for it seemed to him that if Georgiana had been anything other than the minx she surely must be she would have found some way to discourage his suit long before this. But even allowing for the emotional upheaval that Curshawe was undergoing at the moment, the fellow was behaving badly. If he persisted, there was bound to be a scene that would attract the attention of those in the ballroom. He half rose from the bench, just as Curshawe flung the rest of his unfinished sentence at Georgy.

"There *is* someone else, and I know who it is, too! It is Lord Pamyngton!"

It was not this that made Graham pause, but the sound of fresh footsteps approaching. And then he heard another voice, cool and amused, yet with a certain bite in its tone.

"You spoke my name, I think, Curshawe? Is there any way in which I can serve you?"

An uneasy silence fell for a few minutes.

Graham peered through the screen of foliage, anxious now to see what was happening. He could not do more than make out the three figures standing close together, however.

"Miss Georgiana and I were in the middle of a private conversation — " began Curshawe, in a nettled tone.

"Please take me back to the ballroom, Pam!" said Georgy suddenly, in an uncertain voice.

"By all means — that is what I came to do. Your brother Hugh wishes to dance with you, for one thing. By your leave, Curshawe — "

He must have swept out with Georgiana, for Graham heard their retreating footsteps, and saw the solitary figure standing there, muttering curses under his breath.

After a time, Curshawe seemed to pull himself together, and he, too, left the conservatory. Graham jumped up from his seat at once, unwilling to remain any longer in a situation that might again place him in danger of playing the eavesdropper to other embarrassing scenes. His heart was heavy. He had come there trying to reason himself out of the spell which Georgiana Eversley had cast upon him; and even though he told himself that he was leaving with that spell quite broken, he could not feel altogether glad of it.

13

A Reproof From Hugh

GRAHAM had lost all interest in the ball, and would have liked to leave at once. But it was difficult to do so without giving offence, and moreover there was Anne to be considered. While he had been absent, she had been dancing with Freddy Eversley. As soon as her cousin reappeared in the ballroom, she came up to him with sparkling eyes and cheeks flushed with pleasure, saying how much she was enjoying the evening.

"I'm glad of that," he replied, absently. "I find it a bit tedious myself, and was wondering if we might get away before long."

Her face fell, but she tried to conceal her dismay. "If you wish, of course, Cousin John. But won't it appear discourteous if we leave too early? We have no real excuse for doing so."

He gave a twisted smile; he could not bring himself to cut short what he knew was to her a very rare pleasure.

"No, of course not. You are quite right. And if you'll dance with me again, I'm quite sure I shall recover my spirits."

"Of course I will!" She looked gratified at this unexpected compliment, making him feel something of a hypocrite.

So they remained until the end, although they were among the first to go. John Graham partnered a good many of the ladies present, but he did not again ask Georgiana to dance, even though on one occasion she gave him an opportunity to do so. They came face to face during one of the movements of the dance, and were able to exchange a few words. Georgy began the conversation.

"I hope," she said, almost diffidently, "that I did not offend you when I had to refuse to dance with you a little while ago."

"Not at all," he replied, stiffly.

"Oh!" She flashed him an arch smile. "I thought I must have done, for you haven't spoken to me since."

"Really? I hadn't noticed."

He saw the quick flush rise in her cheeks and a momentary pang shot through him. Although at present he was feeling that she thoroughly deserved his offhand treatment, it was hard to mete it out to one so lovely. He might have relented, but the movements of the dance bore her away from him, and the moment was over. He scarcely set eyes on her for the remainder of the evening, although he was hardly conscious of anyone else in the room.

In spite of Graham's abstraction, he did notice that Curshawe was drinking heavily. Towards the end of the evening the now intoxicated man became involved in an incident with Pamyngton which might have turned ugly but for the prompt action of Hugh Eversley.

At the moment when supper was announced, Pamyngton had just finished dancing with Georgiana, and it was natural that he should offer her his arm to lead her into the supper room. But even as he did so, Curshawe, flushed with wine and breathing somewhat heavily, also presented himself at her side. Georgiana, after giving him a look of disgust, turned towards her previous partner. Before she could lay her hand upon Pamyngton's arm, Curshawe thrust him roughly aside.

"Damn you, you shall not take her in!" he grunted menacingly.

Pamyngton raised a delicate eyebrow. "Recollect where you are, my friend," he advised, in a low voice. "This is not a Covent Garden tavern."

"I am no friend of yours," retorted Curshawe, in slurred accents, "and I'll wager you're more often to be found in low taverns than I am! Clear off, for I mean to take Miss Georgy in to supper."

"You're in no state to take any lady in to supper. Go and take a damper, man."

Curshawe drew nearer to Pamyngton, and thrust his heated face close to the other man's. "You say I'm foxed, do you?" He raised his voice, and several people looked round, staring at the group in shocked surprise. "Damme, I'll not stand here and be insulted by such as you! You shall meet me for this — name your seconds, sir!"

198

"Don't be a damned fool," said Pamyngton, softly. "Can't you see you're making a scene? If you have any consideration at all for Miss Eversley, you'll make some effort to behave like a gentleman."

"That's it!" The drunken man was beside himself now. "Add one insult to another! Name your seconds, I say!"

"Curshawe, for God's sake — " began Pamyngton, still keeping his tone low in an effort to diminish the growing attention around them.

"Will you meet me?" The question was almost a shout.

"Of course not — do you suppose I'll allow a man in his cups to call me out? Go and put your head in a bucket of water, there's a good chap."

"Coward!"

Pamyngton's eyes flashed at the word, and his fists clenched automatically. But he kept a strong hold on himself; and, withdrawing from the angry face that was thrust close to his, he turned to offer his arm to Georgiana again. Curshawe whipped round, almost lost his balance, then righted himself and grabbed at

Pamyngton's arm.

"Coward, I say! You'll fight with me, even if I have to force you to it — like this!"

He raised his fist to smash it into his rival's face.

At that moment, his wrist was seized in an iron grip and his body jerked round suddenly. He looked up with a fierce, though hazy expression, and found himself confronting the six foot length of Beau Eversley.

"My dear Curshawe," said Hugh, in soothing accents. "You are not well. Fortunately, we have a medical man among us." Without relaxing his grip on the inebriated Curshawe, he turned to address Graham, who at the time was standing only a few feet away. "If you would be so good, my dear fellow — our friend here is feeling the heat a trifle, I fancy, and is quite dizzy. If we could help him into another room, perhaps you could do something to alleviate his symptoms. I am sorry to trouble you, but you see how it is. My brother George will assist you."

By this time both Hugh's brothers

had noticed the disturbance, and had quickly ranged themselves at his side. Graham nodded in brief understanding, and moved forward to join them.

"Not go with you," muttered Curshawe, obstinately, but with less fire. "Don't want any damned medico — spechully not that one! Won't go an' leave that Pam'ton fellow to take Miss Georgy into supper — "

"No," agreed Hugh, smoothly, releasing Curshawe and drawing Georgiana's arm, which was now trembling slightly, through his. "I myself intend to lead my sister in to supper. Will that satisfy you? Now will you go, like a good chap? You are not at all the thing, you know."

Curshawe's face took on a slightly mollified look. "Right as a trivet," he protested, feebly. "But I'll go to oblige you — my host, after all — can't be uncivil to one's host — "

His voice tailed off into silence. Graham and George Eversley, who had moved one to each side of him as soon as Hugh relaxed his grip, quickly took an arm each and led the now subdued man quietly away.

Pamyngton let out a long breath. "Phew! you arrived in the nick of time, Beau. I could do nothing with the besotted fool, and it was all I could manage not to lose my own temper."

The guests who had so lately been staring now recollected the rules of good breeding, and turned to go into the supper room. Hugh wheeled Georgy round to join them.

"You managed superbly, Pam," he approved. "As for Curshawe, although I deplore his behaviour, I must allow him a certain provocation." He glanced severely at his sister as he spoke.

"Oh, it was dreadful!" shuddered Georgiana, trying to ignore her brother's look. "I am so thankful that Susan had retired early, and that Mrs. Curshawe and Caroline were right at the other end of the room, and cannot have noticed anything! I can't understand it — he is such a very proper man as a rule — scarcely the kind to make a scene in any circumstances, one would think! Of course, I know he was inebriated — "

"Yes, Georgy," agreed her brother, giving her another stern, serious look.

"But why? As you say, he is normally a temperate, even a formal man, unwilling to flout any of the conventions, or draw any attention down upon himself. Yet such a man suddenly makes an unpleasant scene among a crowd of people. I ask you again — why?"

"Oh, how should I know?" asked Georgy, petulantly. "I suppose he wouldn't be the first man who was unable to hold his liquor! Stop quizzing me, Hugh, and let us go in!"

"Very well. But you and I are going to have a serious talk, my girl, before you're very much older."

She shrugged this off, and made a point of being especially gay and lively during supper. But after the ball was over, and the last carriage had rolled away, Hugh drew her aside from the house guests. Curshawe had long since been put to bed, and most of the others were smothering yawns as one by one they bade their host good night. Only Pamyngton lingered at the foot of the staircase, eyeing Hugh speculatively as he guided Georgiana towards the library.

"Good night, Pam," said Hugh

pleasantly, but with an air of finality.

"Oh — er — good night, Beau." Pamyngton accepted his dismissal in good part. "Good night, Miss Georgy."

Georgiana replied in a subdued voice, and allowed her brother to shepherd her into the library. Once there, he nodded towards two chairs which stood before a dying fire, and sat down in one himself.

"It's not worth having this fire made up," he remarked, as Georgy sank into the other chair with an air of fatigue. "We shan't be here long, and the room is warm enough. You don't feel cold?"

"Quite the contrary," said Georgy, wielding her fan. "It was too warm everywhere else — the ballroom was beyond anything! But I'm fagged to death, Hugh. What do you want to say? Whatever it is, pray be brief, or I shall fall asleep here, I warn you!"

"Very well, I'll be brief." His unsmiling face made her heart sink. She was very fond of this eldest brother of hers, and had always paid more heed to him than she had to anyone else in her family circle. "Georgiana, I've reluctantly come to the conclusion that you're a minx."

She snapped her fan shut, and half rose from the chair. "Oh, well, if you've only brought me here in order to call me names — "

"Sit down!" Rarely had she heard him so stern. "I'll give you a chance to defend yourself in a moment — if you can! Meanwhile, you can listen to me." He looked into the green-flecked eyes which were so like his own. "Ever since you left that deuced full seminary of yours, Georgy, you've been attracting the attentions of men, eligible and ineligible. How many is it who've already proposed marriage to you — six?"

"If you count Walter Shayne asking me twice," replied Georgy, with a mocking smirk that was very far from displaying her real feelings, "it's seven."

"Seven. You're prodigiously hard to please, it seems," he said dryly.

"Oh, really, Hugh, I don't see why I should have to take this from you, as well as Sue! She is for ever going on at me about getting married, as though no woman could be happy in the single state!"

"You know why that is. Susan and I

are happy together, and her generous heart cannot bear to see you excluded from a similar happiness."

"It's different for you and Susan," retorted Georgy impatiently. "You are in love — why, even now, after four years of marriage, you quite dote on each other. But I'm not in love with anyone — in fact, I find most of the men I know tedious, to say the least! Not for anything would I tie myself down to one of them!"

"I feel tempted to challenge that statement; but I shan't do so, because I didn't start this conversation with any idea of pressing you into marriage with any one at all. What I wished to say was this — that until lately, I had always believed that the admiration you aroused was not deliberately sought by you, but came unsought as a tribute to your charms, which were completely unstudied."

She stared at him. "Well?"

"I have reason to think otherwise now — and that is why I called you a minx, Georgiana. You've changed lately and I don't care for the change."

A faint flush came into her face. "What do you mean? What reason? What are you accusing me of?"

"Of coquetry of the most contemptible kind. Of leading men on to think you serious, when your only object is to amuse yourself at their expense."

"Oh la! You're grown very prudish, all of a sudden," she mocked. "Why, what did you do before you were wed but flirt with every pretty girl in Town? And now you censure me for doing the same kind of thing — not that I admit it, mind, for I don't!"

"Heaven knows I wouldn't wish you to follow my example in anything," he said frowning. "And at least I never aroused any expectations which I had no intention of fulfilling. The ladies concerned fully understood the rules of the game."

"There was at least one who didn't," retorted Georgy, triumphantly, "and you can't deny it, Hugh! All the Town know that Barbara Radley almost went into a decline when you transferred your attentions from her to someone else!"

She saw with satisfaction that he looked

a shade disconcerted for a moment; but the expression was soon gone, to be replaced by an even sterner look than he had worn before.

"It's no good, Georgy. You won't side-track me by launching into a catalogue of *my* past faults. We are concerned with *your* present ones. Do you wish to get a name for being the most accomplished flirt in Polite Society? If so, you are going the right way about it."

"But what am I supposed to have done?" she asked, in exasperated tones. "Only tell me that, Hugh!"

"I have told you. And even if I hadn't mentioned it, your conscience must have told you that the distressing scene we were forced to undergo just before supper was entirely due to your encouragement of that poor devil Curshawe!"

"Well, if that doesn't surpass every-thing!" exclaimed Georgy, indignantly. "Can I help it if the silly creature takes too much to drink, and makes a fool of himself as a result? Far from encouraging him — as you accuse me — I have been trying to depress his pretensions ever since he came to stay with us in the country! I am heartily sick of the way he goes on, and so is Pam!"

"Then why did you go with him alone into the conservatory earlier this evening? You are not a little schoolroom miss, Georgy, so you must know very well that any man would consider that a most particular form of encouragement."

Her eyes dropped away from his. "Yes, of course I do. But the fact is that I knew" — she looked up again defiantly — "I knew he meant to propose to me some time, and I thought I might as well get it over and done with there and then, and afterwards perhaps he would let me alone! I've been driven near distracted trying to prevent him from getting the chance to be private with me, and suddenly I decided that after all it was better to let him pop the question, and have his answer once for all!"

"I see. Perhaps I've misjudged you on that head," he said, slowly. "I do see your point of view — it is in your character to get a thing over and done with quickly when you can see no way of avoiding it. But can you honestly say that you haven't been leading the man on lately?"

She shook her head vehemently. "Never! why, it isn't even as though there's any *fun* to be had out of flirting with him! He takes everything so seriously!"

"The poor devil will take this night's affair seriously enough, when he's sufficiently sober to recollect what a cake he made of himself. Tell you the truth, I'm expecting him to remember an urgent engagement in London in the morning."

"I hope he does go — he's the most stupid, boring man I know," said Georgy with a yawn, rising to her feet. "I'm going to bed, Hugh, if you've done."

"Not quite," he said. "I'll allow that possibly I've misjudged you as far as Curshawe's concerned. But what of your conduct towards this other man, this medical friend of George's? You'll have to talk very hard to convince me that you've not been playing the minx with him."

"George's friend?" She sounded surprised, but he noticed the faint colour that came up in her cheeks.

"Yes. Come, my dear, I'm not such a

fool as you take me for. I'm speaking — as you very well know — of Dr. Graham. I've been watching your conduct with him of late, and I've come to a settled conclusion that you're doing your best to entrap him."

"Fustian!" she retorted, hastily. "Why, everyone knows that I detest the man — we are always at odds, he and I, as Susan will tell you."

"What Susan has told me, together with things I've observed for myself, have led me to form my present opinion. Why you are playing the coquette with him, I can't pretend to guess. I should have supposed there were men enough in your own circle, if you wish to try that kind of game — men who know the rules, and who wouldn't allow themselves to get hurt. But if you do succeed in snaring this quarry, Georgiana, it will do you scant credit, and him a great deal of harm. I like the man — he's a good chap, as George says, and seems to be a clever man at his job. He's too good, my girl, to be made a fool of by you. Don't distract him any further with your pretended favours, but leave him to make

211

a match of it with that charming little cousin of his, who is eminently suited to him in every way."

He rose, and put an arm about her shoulders, smiling down into her face. "Come, little sister, I can see you're in a pet with me, but don't get on your high horse. I cannot bear to see you acting in a way that is contrary to the best in your nature. You're too honest to find any true satisfaction in deception, and too kind-hearted to enjoy hurting others. Be yourself — your true self — that's all I ask. What need have you to seek admiration? It's always been yours for the taking."

She made no reply, and when he looked closely into her face, he saw that her eyes were swimming in tears. He gave her a pat, and guided her towards the door.

"Silly puss," he said, gently. "Why can't you make your mind up to marry Pam? You would deal famously together, you two."

14

The Morning After

ON the following morning more than one person felt the effects of the previous evening's events. Curshawe slept late, waking in the middle of the morning with a thick head and a general feeling of unease, physical and mental. Something had gone badly wrong last night, he was sure, but he could not at first recollect what it was. He puzzled over it a little while he made himself ready to go downstairs, but his head was aching too much for him to persist, and his manservant, who could have helped him, was silent.

Evidently he was not the only one to rise late; when he entered the breakfast parlour, he found several other members of the party assembled there. They gave him a wary look, but he was not in a sufficiently perceptive state to notice this. He sat down heavily, accepted a cup of coffee, and waved away offers of food with a pained expression. Freddy, who was sitting next to him, leaned over confidentially.

"I know the very best thing for your trouble," he said grinning. "Tell you what, I'll fix it up for you now, if you like to go into the library — that's if Hugh ain't there. Dare say you won't care to meet him just yet, eh?"

"I'd be obliged, Frederick, if you wouldn't talk in riddles," replied Curshawe, passing a hand over his eyes. "I don't seem at all the thing this morning."

Freddy laughed. "Not surprising, old chap. Bit up in the boughs last night, weren't you? Never mind — I tell you I can soon fix that for you, if you come with me."

"Up in the — ?" Curshawe turned to stare at his neighbour. "Are you suggesting I was inebriated?" he asked in tones of horror.

Freddy nodded. "Tight as an owl. Completely castaway, give you my word. Don't you remember?"

Curshawe shook his head, then winced. "No. But I had a feeling there was something wrong — "

"Come on," said Freddy, rising from the table. "I'd better give you some idea of how the land lies, I can see."

Curshawe gulped down a mouthful of coffee, and rose to follow him.

"Here, drink this," said Freddy, about five minutes later, coming into the library where he had settled Curshawe, and holding out a glass.

"What is it?" asked Curshawe, suspiciously.

"Oh, a little concoction of my own for a thick head. It'll set you right in no time — you'll see. Go on, gulp it down, man, it won't harm you."

Having first smelt the liquid, Curshawe obediently swallowed it, then made a wry face.

"If you're playing off one of your jokes on me — " he began, indignantly.

"No, no — I assure you, it's all right. Never kick a man when he's down," protested Freddy. "Do you mean to say, though, Curshawe, that you don't recollect anything of what took place yesterday evening?"

Curshawe put his head in his hands. "I

didn't," he replied, with a groan, "but it's coming back to me now. There was an argument with Pamyngton — something to do with your sister — oh, God!"

Freddy regarded him with something close to sympathy. He had no use for Curshawe, but the man was in an awkward situation, and Freddy's sporting instincts prompted him to lend a hand. Besides, it would be no bad thing for everybody if Curshawe decided to curtail his visit, and once he realized what a fool he had made of himself last night, surely he would go as soon as possible?

"That's about it," Freddy said, helpfully. "George and his friend Jock Graham towed you off and tucked you up in bed — –"

"Oh, God!" exclaimed Curshawe again. "I — I believe I tried to call Pamyngton out, didn't I? And then your brother Hugh came along — " He broke off, and looked at Freddy wildly. "What the devil can I do about it?" he continued, in tones of despair.

Freddy shrugged. "Best forgotten. Tell you, you were completely castaway. They know it — they won't take it seriously, you'll see."

"But I take it seriously!" burst out Curshawe. "And when I consider what Miss Georgiana must think of me — "

It was on the tip of Freddy's tongue to advise his companion not to worry on that score, either, as Georgy had never had any good opinion of him to lose. But he kept quiet, contenting, himself with another shrug.

"I must go to them at once!" went on Curshawe, in an agitated tone. He half rose from his seat, then subsided with a groan.

"You'd far better just sit quiet here, and give that potion time to do the trick," advised Freddy.

Curshawe groaned again. "Perhaps so. But afterwards I must at once seek out your brother and sister, and make them my apologies! I can scarcely stay under Hugh's roof, after this — he must wish me gone already! As for Pamyngton — "

"Oh, Lord, don't put yourself into a taking over Pam," said Freddy, carelessly. "He ain't the man to bear a grudge — especially as he knew you were foxed. Well, we all did, come to that. No mistaking it."

"What you say only fills me with a deep repugnance for my own behaviour," said Curshawe, in bitterly humiliated tones. "To think that Miss Georgy should have seen me behaving in a fashion that — that — "He could not continue.

Freddy flung him a half contemptuous look. "Well, no use overdoing the self-loathing stuff. Thing is, you did make a bit of a cake of yourself. Not the first time a man's done anything of the kind, though, when he'd taken more than was good for him. My advice is, apologize to Hugh — after all, he's your host — then forget about it. Least said soonest mended. Why not take a turn in the grounds, when you feel more the thing? Nothing like fresh air to blow the cobwebs away."

★ ★ ★

Georgiana was also trying the effects of fresh air on jaded spirits. She had breakfasted early, and slipped away to walk alone along a path which ran right round the grounds to the boundary wall

218

which separated Fulmer Towers from the road.

It was a golden October morning, and at any other time she would have delighted in the glowing tints of the trees which stood on either side of the path, their autumn colours set off by the background of a delicate blue sky. Trees had always had the power to move her quick sense of beauty. But today she did not see the trees, and walked unheeding past the bright piles of gold and amber leaves which the gardeners had heaped beside the path, ready for burning. What had happened last night had in some way left her changed; but how and why, was at present beyond her understanding. She walked along with bent head, trying to solve the riddle.

Her abstraction was broken at last by the sound of a horse trotting along the road on the other side of the wall. She stood listening for a moment, then an old childhood impulse came over her to see who it was. Close to the wall not far from this point there had been a sawn-off tree trunk which she had often used as a look-out post. She ran towards it now, and scrambled on to its broad, flat surface. In the old days, she had been obliged to stand on tiptoe to see over the wall from her vantage point; now she found herself standing head and shoulders above the wall, with a clear view of the road below.

The rider was approaching from her right and was at first hidden from view by the trees which grew beside the wall. In a few moments, he drew level with the spot where she was standing, and then she saw that it was John Graham. Involuntarily she gave a little gasp of surprise which drew his attention. He turned his head in her direction; their eyes were almost on a level, and as their glance met, he drew rein sharply. The horse fidgeted for a moment before responding to his capable hands.

He removed his hat, and bowed curtly. "Good morning."

"Good morning," replied Georgy, with a welcoming smile. She hesitated a moment, then, seeing that he was about to ride on, exclaimed impetuously, "Oh, no, pray don't go! Stay and talk to me for a while — I'm in the doldrums this morning."

"Are you?" he asked, without any noticeable interest. "Perhaps late evenings do not suit you."

She forced a laugh. "They should — I have sufficient of them in Town!"

"No doubt. Well, I do not. And I fear, Miss Eversley, that in consequence you'd find me rather poor company at present. So I'll be on my way."

"Oh, no, please!" she pleaded, leaning over the wall so that her tawny curls fell forward on to her face. "Even poor company's better than none — and I can't bear my own at present!"

His dark eyes looked bleakly into her green ones. "You've plenty of company in the house," he said curtly.

"Those people!" She tossed the hair back from her face. "I am heartily sick of them all — yes, even my dear little Sue, who never did any harm to anyone!"

"They may be equally sick of you," he suggested, grimly.

She shrugged. "Possibly — very likely. One always grows tired of house parties after a time. It's all diverting enough at first; and then all at once everything and everyone seems prodigiously boring! I think I've been too long away from London — it's time I returned."

"Yes, perhaps that would be best," he replied in a voice devoid of expression.

She stared at him for a moment, then asked abruptly, "Where are you going? Are you in a hurry?"

He shook his head, and glanced at the road ahead. "I'm exercising this horse for a patient of mine who's broken his leg — or, at least, that's his way of putting it. He's urged me to borrow the animal whenever I've a mind, but this is the first time I've taken him at his word. Today I felt I wanted a canter, and poor old Nell's past it."

"But George told you he'd find you a mount at any time from our stable," protested Georgy.

"Maybe," replied Graham. "But I don't choose to be under an obligation to your brother."

"Oh, don't be absurd!" She reached out a hand towards him across the wall. "Look here, won't you come in and finish this conversation? There's a gate in the wall just a little way down there, by the way you've just come — I'll go and let you in."

He seemed about to refuse, but she gave him no chance, for she disappeared promptly. Jumping down from the tree trunk, she pattered quickly through the fallen leaves until she reached a side gate which she unbolted and flung open. He was already waiting on the other side. He dismounted and led the horse through in silence.

"Perhaps you'll tether your horse to that post," she suggested, turning to fasten the gate so that she could cover a momentary embarrassment. "Would you like to go up to the house and join the others? Or shall we walk along this path a little way? That is what I was doing when I saw you."

"I must not stay long, in any case," he replied, rather stiffly. "So perhaps I won't go up to the house."

She turned to continue her walk, and he fell into step beside her. Nothing was said for a few moments. On either side, there was a sense of unspoken thoughts which weighed heavily on the spirits.

"How is your arm?" he asked politely, at last.

She gave an impatient shrug. "Oh, that is quite healed — you know better than anyone that it was nothing! I don't wish to talk of that!"

"Don't you?" he asked, with one of his twisted smiles. "Then be good enough to tell me what you do wish to talk of, and I'll do my best to oblige you."

"Oh, anything and nothing!" She flashed an answering smile at him. "For a start, you can tell me why you won't let George oblige you in the matter of a horse."

"'Neither a borrower nor a lender be'," he quoted, swiftly.

She screwed up her face. "Pooh! Polonius! And he was a dreary old bore, if ever Shakespeare created one!"

He glanced at her mockingly. "So young English ladies do receive the rudiments of an education, at any rate," he remarked. "I am surprised to find it. Now in Scotland, of course, it is quite another matter."

"Oho!" She chuckled, and gave him an arch look. "I suppose every goose is

224

a swan in Scotland, and every milkmaid can recite the poets — is that so, sir? I wonder you could ever bring yourself to quit a place where the females are so exactly what you would wish! I declare you must be vastly disappointed in what you have found south of the Border!"

He turned towards her, and her dancing green eyes met his, which today appeared more serious than usual. And then he felt again the sensation which had overcome him yesterday in the ballroom; as their eyes met, it seemed as if their spirits leapt up together in wild ecstasy.

"Georgy!" His voice was hoarse.

She lowered her gaze. Strange flutterings were going on inside her, and she could not trust herself to speak.

"I've got to tell you," he said, still in the same strained tone. "You must know the truth now — all of it."

He paused for a moment, evidently struggling for control over his feelings. When he spoke again, his voice was calmer, more normal. "There was a moment last night, in the ballroom, when I looked at you across the room — "

"I know," she said, softly, not daring to look up at him.

He stared at her for a moment, then started forward impetuously. She stood still, waiting with quickened pulses.

But suddenly he drew back, smashing a clenched fist down on the open palm of his other hand in a violent gesture.

"Yes, you know!" he echoed, in bitter tones. "You also know that afterwards when I came to dance with you, you refused me in favour of that poor devil Curshawe. And then, like the accomplished coquette you are, you wheedled him into the conservatory alone with you, until finally he ended up by making you an offer which, needless to say, you never had the slightest intention of accepting!" She started at this, and he went on ruthlessly, "Yes, I know all about it, you see! I heard every word that passed between you. I was already in the conservatory when you both came out there. You didn't see me, because I was on a nearby seat, shielded from view by the greenery."

A look of scorn crossed her face. "Eavesdropping! How low can you sink?"

"Not yet as low as you," he replied coldly. "It was accidental. I came out after you refused to dance with me — I wanted to think. And then before I had time to do anything about it, you and he were there, and he was declaring himself to you. I could scarcely step out in front of you at that stage — there was nothing for it but to sit tight until you had gone."

"A *gentleman* would not have listened!" she exclaimed, scathingly.

"Perhaps not, and to do myself justice, I tried to avoid it — for a time, at least. But you were both too close to me, for one thing — for another — " He broke off.

"Well? For another — " she prompted.

"Oh, God!" he burst out, explosively. "You know very well what the other reason was! How could I close my ears, when another man was telling you the things that — "

"Yes?" Her voice softened.

"Oh, Georgy! How could you lead that man on to declare his love for you? I realized before that you were selfish and wilful — "

"Thank you very much!" she exclaimed, all her softness vanishing.

" . . . but I never knew what an accomplished flirt you were! I thought that men flocked round you because of your irresistible loveliness — and, by God, you *are* lovely, Georgiana! — but last night I saw that you deliberately angled for their attentions. I suppose it panders to your vanity — it's a very interesting example of the mating instinct in the female — "

She wheeled on him, her eyes glinting with green fire. "Your conversation disgusts me!" she cried, fiercely. "Must you pin everyone's character down on your dissecting table? You shall not do so with mine, I promise you! Or if you do, I shall not stay to hear it! I wish you good day, Dr. Graham!"

With a swish of skirts, she turned away and almost ran along the path in the direction of the house.

"No, wait!" He caught her up in a few quick strides, and taking her arm, turned her towards him. Her face was flushed with anger, her shining hair was tumbled, and tears stood in her eyes. He stood looking down at her for a moment, his expressive eyes staring into hers. As he looked, all the barriers between them seemed to melt away. She closed her eyes and swayed towards him. Suddenly she was held close in his arms, and he was kissing her as though this was the last thing he might do before the world came to an end.

15

Brief Ecstasy

AFTER a while, she placed her hand on his chest, and held him a little away from her.

"Jock." She spoke his name shyly. "You were wrong, you know. It wasn't like that."

"My darling." He placed his lips close to her ear. "What wasn't like what?"

"Mr. Curshawe." He made an impatient movement, and started to draw her close to him again. She held him off, gently but firmly. "No, you must listen. Hugh also accused me of leading Mr. Curshawe on, but I made him see that it was unjust — and so must you see it. I did not want him to — to — fall in love with me" — her voice faltered a little — "but in spite of that he did, and then — and then — well, he pestered me so! There was no bearing it, and I could see it would never be any better until I had allowed him to declare himself, and I'd rejected his offer." She was about to say that she had found this the best way of dealing with importunate suitors in the past, but she thought better of it at the last moment. "So that was why I allowed him to take me into the conservatory," she concluded. "Of course, I know it wasn't exactly *proper*, but it seemed the best way to get it over and done with as soon as possible. You *must* see that, Jock — " She paused, looking anxiously at him. "You do see, don't you? Only say you understand!"

He had listened attentively to the latter part of her speech, and now he nodded. "Yes, I do see, my darling. But let's forget about that now, and think what is to be done about ourselves — you and I."

"Why, what is there to think about?" she asked with a little smile.

"I must go up to London and see your father, for one thing." He frowned. "I can't flatter myself that he'll precisely favour my suit."

"Why not? I find you suitable, and that should suffice."

"Darling — my lovely girl!" He drew her close again for a moment, then put her resolutely aside. "But we must give this some serious thought. At present, I have little to offer in comparison with others who seek your hand. One day, I shall be Laird of Kinwiddie, and able to make you mistress of a castle with one of the loveliest views in Scotland — and that is to say a great deal. By that time, I hope — nay, I am determined" — he threw back his dark head defiantly — "that I shall also be of some account in my chosen profession. But all that is in the future, and at present I am an obscure medico with only a small independent income. For the rest, I must depend upon my own efforts. I realize that this can hardly be considered good enough for one who aspires to the hand of an Eversley."

"Fudge!" she said energetically. "As to fortune, I have enough for us both."

He shook his head. "I want none of it. If we must have it, it shall be exclusively yours. But I had rather take you without a penny."

"Well, perhaps Papa could be persuaded

to disinherit me," she suggested, quizzically. "I wonder if I could manage to sustain a life in straitened circumstances? Certainly I've had no practice at it."

He smiled, but shook his head. "Don't jest, my love. Although we may think little of such things, your family will set great store by them, we may depend. And who can blame them? They have your interest very much at heart. Perhaps," he added, thoughtfully, "the only truly chivalrous course for me would to step out of your life."

"Useless," replied Georgy, "I should follow you."

"Could you possibly be so unmaidenly?" he teased her.

"Much, much more than that! Just you wait and see! My conduct has always been the despair of my mentors!"

"You are completely adorable to me," he said, in a low voice, holding her to him in a sudden grip that almost made her wince. "There could be no one like you — ever — and I must have you — or no one . . . "

A fluttering sigh escaped her as his lips met hers. For a moment, time seemed to stand still. So engrossed were they in each other, that they failed to hear in time the footsteps of two people approaching through the trees.

The next moment, Curshawe and Freddy were standing before them on the path.

"Good God!" exclaimed Freddy, in tones of horror.

Curshawe said nothing, staring as though he could scarcely believe his eyes. Georgy and Graham started apart, though he still retained his grip on her hand. He met the other men's stares with a look of challenge.

"Come on, Curshawe, this is no place for us!" said Freddy, at last, turning on his heel.

Curshawe came to life with a start, and also turned away.

"No, stop!" commanded Graham. The others slowly turned about again. "You may as well know," he went on, addressing Freddy, "that your sister has just consented to become my wife."

Freddy whistled, staring. "Well, I'm damned!" was all he could find to say.

"Possibly," replied Graham, dryly.

"But at least you could wish us happy."

Freddy appeared confused for a moment. "Oh, well — yes," he stammered, "so I would, if I thought — that's to say — " He broke off, and turned on his sister with some show of temper. "Damme, Georgy, what the devil d'you mean by letting things get as far as this? There was no need to delude the chap into thinking you were in earnest — "

"You don't understand — " began Georgy, but Graham cut her short.

"What are you talking about?" he asked, looking suspiciously from brother to sister, and noting the slow flush that was spreading over Georgiana's face.

"Oh, Lord, I don't know!" muttered Freddy, with a hang dog air. "You'd best ask her yourself. Come on, Curshawe."

He dragged imperatively at the other man's arm, but Curshawe shook him off. A cold anger was showing in his face.

"I'll tell you what Frederick is talking about," he said, with a sneer. "He's remembering a little wager he had with his sister not long since." He turned to Freddy. "It looks as though you've lost Frederick — a pity. Still, the odds were weighted against you, you must realize."

"Shut your mouth!" growled Freddy, inelegantly

"Come," mocked Curshawe, now maliciously enjoying himself, "where is the famous Eversley charm? It hasn't failed to win Miss Georgiana her bet, though, has it? But then, who could resist so lovely a lady?"

Freddy turned fiercely on him, but was forestalled by Graham, who suddenly sprang forward, seizing Curshawe in a relentless grip.

"Damn you!" he muttered, between clenched teeth. "What are you trying to insinuate? Out with it, straight — before I do you a mischief!"

"Let him go, Jock!" cried Georgy, tugging at Graham's sleeve. "I'll explain everything — "

He shook her off. "I'm going to hear what he has to say, first! Now, Curshawe — " He tightened his hold on the man.

Curshawe released an oath. "I'll tell you, right enough. It will be a pleasure. But let go of me, first."

"If you breathe a word, Curshawe,"

threatened Freddy, clenching his fists, "I'll make mincemeat of you, so help me!"

"Oh, Jock!" pleaded Georgy. "Pray don't listen to him! — I'll explain, I tell you — "

Graham ignored them both completely. He released Curshawe, giving him a shake as he did so. "Now talk!" he commanded, tersely.

Curshawe tugged at his cravat with a trembling hand, and tried desperately to assume an expression of nonchalance.

"Nothing easier," he said. "The fact is, that Miss Georgiana has led you up the garden path. She has no intention of wedding you, nor ever did have. She was simply trying to win a wager which she had with Frederick here — "

Freddy and Georgy both tried to break in at this point, but Graham silenced them with a curt command. "What was the nature of this wager?"

"Simply that Miss Georgiana undertook to make you fall in love with her during the time you were here in the country. If she failed, she was to pay her brother a sum of money — " he broke off, and inquiringly turned towards Freddy, who was watching him with loathing. "I forget the precise amount?"

"You are the lowest thing in nature!" said Georgy, in a voice trembling with emotion.

Curshawe bowed. "I know you have no very high opinion of me, ma'am. I discovered that yesterday evening. But at least no one can accuse me of trying to give a false impression, of raising hopes which I have no intention of fulfilling — in short, of trifling with another's feelings." He bowed. "I'm leaving your house today, so I'll bid you farewell. I know you will all of you be glad to see me gone."

He walked quickly away in the direction of the house. The others stood silent for several minutes, staring after him. Georgy was the first to break the silence, flinging herself on Graham with hot tears starting to her eyes.

"Jock! My dear! Only let me tell you the whole — "

He put her away from him. His face was white, but completely devoid of expression.

"You have told me enough lies," he said harshly. "Have done — you've won your bet — what more do you want?"

"I'll leave you to sort it out," muttered Freddy, turning away. "My God! Just wait until I catch up with that fellow!"

They did not heed him. They stood facing each other; they were not more than a foot apart, but now worlds seemed to divide them.

"You must let me explain, Jock — "

He laughed mirthlessly. "Explain? Explain how you cajoled me, and tricked me, all for your own amusement, because a wager lends some zest to the uneventful life of the country? Oh, yes, you'll explain right enough — and I might be fool enough to believe you again! No, thank you! I've been caught in that trap once, and I don't mean to repeat the experience! I know you now positively for a heartless flirt, without conscience or scruple, who will use men's hearts as toys for your amusement. I can only thank God for a lucky escape! If you had truly wished to become my wife, what kind of existence would have lain before me? I should have been the dupe of your whims, the victim of your selfishness, for the rest of my life. I am well rid of you, madam. I hope I may never see you again as long as I live."

He whipped round and striding towards the spot where he had tethered his horse, led it out of the gate. She heard the gate closing, and afterwards the quick tattoo of galloping hoofs along the road.

He had gone.

16

Georgy In London

A FEW days later, Georgiana was back in London. Susan had raised a little protest at her going.

"I did hope that you'd be here to see the new baby," she objected, gently. "It's less than a month now."

"Oh, I'll return in time for that, never fear!" replied Georgy. "But I must get away just now, Sue — you know how it is with me — I can never stay long in one place, or I get a fit of the megrims!"

Susan studied her sister-in-law thoughtfully. Georgy was pacing up and down in a flutter of skirts, her hands moving restlessly, her face unnaturally pale and with a strained look about the eyes.

"What's amiss, love? There's something wrong, I know. Tell me what it is."

Georgy shrugged impatiently. "Nothing, but that I need a change of scene — and people — though I don't mean you and

241

Hugh, of course," she added, quickly, seeing the hurt look on Susan's face.

"Is it because of the fuss Henry Curshawe made yesterday evening at the ball? Surely not! The Curshawes are leaving us this afternoon, in any case, so then we shall be a pleasant family party, apart from the Radleys and dear Pam, whom you go on with so well."

"How do you know about the scene last night?"

"Hugh told me, of course."

A line of bitterness showed around Georgy's mouth. "Then I suppose he also told you that it was all my fault?"

"Well — " began Susan, slowly.

"I don't doubt he said that I am an incorrigible flirt, who deliberately goes out of her way to play havoc with poor, suffering men's hearts!" exclaimed Georgy bitterly, her cheeks flushing.

"He wasn't quite as severe as that. He did say" — Susan sought in her mind for words to soften her husband's criticisms — "that you had perhaps been a little injudicious in your behaviour towards Mr. Curshawe — "

She broke off abruptly. Georgy eyed her suspiciously.

"Is that all?"

"N-no," admitted Susan, reluctantly. "Not quite. He did mention another person — "

"Dr. Graham?" Georgy flung up her head defiantly. "Well, you may as well know, Sue, that I *did* encourage Jock Graham." She laughed mirthlessly as she saw the shocked look on her sister-in-law's gentle face. "And you may as well know, too — for there'll be others to tell you, if I don't — that I did it solely for a wager I entered into with Freddy!"

Susan could make no answer to this for a time, but sat staring at Georgy as though she doubted the evidence of her ears.

"You needn't look so shocked — it only seemed a bit of harmless sport at the time. And, anyway," went on Georgy defensively, "he deserved taking down a peg! You surely can't have forgotten the abominable way he treated me over that collision — I swore then I would get even with him, and now I have!"

"But surely the punishment is out of

all proportion to the offence," said Susan, slowly, a troubled expression in her eyes. "You know, Georgy, I have been thinking for some time that — that he was falling in love with you; and I felt sorry for him, because I know from experience that it's a very melancholy thing to be in love with someone who doesn't care for you."

"Well, you need feel no more pity for him," replied Georgy, with set lips. "He has quite recovered now from any tenderness he may have formerly felt towards me — he knows about the wager, and holds me in the utmost contempt, I assure you."

"Did you tell him about the wager yourself?" asked Susan, trying to fathom Georgy's manner.

"No. Henry Curshawe did, in a fit of spite. Freddy was fool enough to let him and Pam into the secret some days since — if you recall, I told you that I was mad with Freddy for betraying a confidence of mine, though I wouldn't tell you precisely what it was — "

Susan nodded. "Yes, I do remember about that, because it worried me at the time."

"Well, after all that happened last night, I think Mr. Curshawe feels he owes me a grudge — though heaven knows, I swear to you, Sue, I never once encouraged that man! — anyway, when I was out walking this morning, we all chanced to come together — that's to say, Dr. Graham — " She stumbled a little over the name, and Susan eyed her sharply. "Freddy and Henry Curshawe — " She broke off, shrugging her shoulders and Susan could see how close the tears were.

"That was when Curshawe told — told about the wager," she concluded, shakily. "Anyway, talking pays no toll! I dare say George won't wish to remain here, if Curshawe leaves for Town this afternoon. Perhaps he will drive me back tomorrow."

She bent over and kissed Susan warmly on the cheek. "I'm sorry, Sue — I must go away. I can't stay here — now. But I'll be back again before your confinement, trust me."

Susan realized that Georgy's mind was quite made up, and there was no hope of changing it. As Georgy had expected, her brother was eager to return to Town on the heels of his affianced, and so it was settled that he should take Georgy back with him on the following day.

A pile of invitations to balls, routs, masquerades and evening parties of every description awaited Georgiana on her return. She proceeded to accept them all, plunging headlong into a fever of social activity which left her no time for thought. She made the usual discovery that she had nothing to wear to these occasions, in spite of the contrary evidence of several overflowing wardrobes standing against the walls of her bedchamber.

Pulling out gown after gown, and flinging each one pettishly down, she overwhelmed her maid Stevens by presenting the girl with most of the tumbled finery before setting out for Bond St., with the intention of starting afresh.

"Lord love us!" exclaimed Stevens, her bright eyes almost popping out of her head as she picked up her haul after her mistress had gone. "If Miss Georgy in't in a powerful paddy, indeed to goodness! But there, it's an ill wind blows no good to nobody, yes, it is indeed!"

Frequent forays in Bond St. over the next few days did a great deal to repair Georgy's humour. No woman can entirely resist the restoring influence of something new to wear. Moreover, she was not the only one whose spirits benefited from her shopping spree. Madame Picot, proprietress of the exclusive dress shop which Georgy patronized, came very near to dancing a jig as order succeeded order; and her habitual expression of having a rather bad smell under her nose gave way to something almost approaching enthusiasm.

Georgy left Madame Picot's shop one day and turned to walk towards her carriage, which had been obliged by a press of traffic to wait for her lower down the street. She had taken only a few steps when she almost bumped into three ladies who were coming towards her. She halted momentarily to apologize, and then recognized two of them with surprise.

It was Mrs. Hume and her daughter Anne. They seemed equally surprised to Georgiana. They presented her to the third lady, who turned out to be Mrs. Hume's sister.

"We have been staying with my sister for the last few days," explained Mrs. Hume. "She lives in the village of Islington, and she is for ever asking me to visit her, but when my husband is at home, I can't spare the time, you know. However, Anne wanted a change, so I thought I would bring her."

"I dare say your nephew will miss you both," said Georgy, overcoming a reluctance to refer to Dr. Graham.

"As to that, I am returning this afternoon, for my husband will be home in a few days. But it was John's doing that we came at all, wasn't it Anne?" She looked at her daughter for confirmation, and Anne gave a little nod. "He insisted that he'd be quite all right with Mrs. Chiltern to look after him — she helps me with the housekeeping, you know."

"Can I take you anywhere?" asked Georgy. "My carriage is waiting lower down the street."

"Oh, no, thank you, Miss Eversley. You are very good, but we are just amusing ourselves, strolling round the

Town. We've been in the linen drapers' in the City, and now my sister wanted to show me the fashionable quarter. But we will walk with you to your carriage — that is, if you've nothing else you wish to do."

Georgy accepted their escort, but the pavement was fairly crowded, so they were obliged to walk in pairs, Anne went ahead with her aunt, and Georgy followed with Mrs. Hume.

"Have you been long in London, Miss Eversley? I had no notion you had left Fulmer Towers, for John did not mention it, though he goes there most days now, because Mrs. Eversley's confinement is so close."

"I left over a week since," replied Georgy. "Tell me, how is my sister-in-law? She was very well when last I heard from her."

"She continues so, my dear ma'am — John says that she is a natural mother, and should have no difficulty at all in presenting your brother with a large, healthy family. You can be quite easy about her, I assure you. And my husband will be home in a few days in good time for the confinement, so then you'll know she is in the best possible hands," concluded Mrs. Hume, proudly. "He has brought nearly a hundred babies into the world, ma'am! I always tell John he has a long way to go, yet, to keep pace with his uncle; but my husband thinks very well of John, very well indeed."

Georgy did not know quite what to say to this, but she tried to look her approval. Mrs. Hume's glance travelled ahead to Anne, and a worried frown showed between her eyes.

"It's a pity," she said, with a sigh. "My husband and I would give anything if John and our little Anne were to make a match of it. He's such a fine young man — we've known him since babyhood, and we understand the best and the worst of him, which is more than most parents can possibly hope for in a prospective son-in-law. But I don't know how it is" — she sighed again — "he doesn't seem to regard her as anything but a sister. I fancied he was beginning to, when he had been with us a little time, but lately he scarcely seems to notice her existence. My poor little girl! I fear she's allowed herself to hope — but I mustn't burden you with my troubles, Miss Eversley. Only that was why I thought it might be no bad thing to fetch Anne away for a bit — she is to stay on for a while with my sister, after I return home. And my nephew will most likely be gone before she comes home again, for he won't stay long once my husband is back. Best for Anne, perhaps, if they are parted until he knows his mind in the business. This visit will give her thoughts a new direction, too. Indeed, it is doing so already, for my sister's children are very much of Anne's age, and they are constantly planning some new diversion for her. Tonight they are all to go to the play, and tomorrow there's to be a visit to Ranelagh Gardens. I must own, she seems much more cheerful now than when we arrived, so perhaps it will all blow over. I dare say it is a great mistake for parents to make up their minds whom children will marry, for such things very rarely turn out as one expects."

Georgy would scarcely have known what kind of reply to make, but she was spared the necessity because they had now reached the carriage and caught up with Anne and her aunt. Good-byes were spoken, and Georgy issued a warm invitation to the Humes to visit her at any time in Clarges St. She did not think it would be taken up, however, because Anne Hume, although quite friendly in her manner, was not cordial. Even if her cousin's lack of interest in her had not quite broken her heart, thought Georgy, evidently she could not entirely forgive the woman she knew to be responsible for it.

Georgy took some melancholy thoughts into the carriage with her. There was no end to the mischief that had been done by her ill-chosen wager with Freddy, and it was no use blaming anyone but herself for it. She had been too concerned with her own amusement, too careless of the feelings of everyone else. What had Jock Graham said? "A heartless flirt, without conscience or scruple." Part of it was true.

She entered the house in a sombre mood. A footman approached her as she was starting to climb the stairs to her own room.

252

"Lord Pamyngton is waiting for you in the small parlour, madam."

Georgiana stared. Pam here? She had not expected to see him in Town just yet. When she had left Fulmer Towers, he had said that he meant to stay on and try to sustain Hugh over the time of Susan's confinement. She shrugged; oh, well, everyone had the liberty to change a plan. But she hoped that he had not come away on her account. At the moment, the last thing she wanted was to have a lovesick suitor hanging about her. She smiled ruefully, realizing that this was scarcely fair to Pam. He had always wooed her in the most lighthearted fashion, almost as if it were simply a game to him. That was why she had found his attentions less irksome than those of others — well, of most others. There were some men, of course, whose notion of wooing a girl was to hurl insults at her. She smiled reminiscently, then sighed as she turned in the direction of the parlour.

Pamyngton came to his feet as she entered. He was wearing a dark coat which suited his fair skin and hair, and deepened the blue of his eyes. There was elegance here, she thought suddenly, and it was matched by an equal elegance of mind. She greeted him, and expressed her surprise at seeing him in London. "I thought you meant to stay and cheer Hugh," she said.

"Radley is there, and your younger brother," he replied. "Not to mention your Aunt Lavinia."

Georgy grimaced. "Oh, Aunt Lavinia! I dare say she will drive him mad! I know she affects me in that way."

"I think he will do well enough. Anyway, Buckinghamshire lost all charm for me when you decided to leave it."

She did not want any remarks of this kind, and hastened to change the subject, saying the first thing that came into her head.

"Who do you think I met just now, in Bond St.? Dr. Hume's wife and daughter — they are staying with a relative in Islington."

He raised his brows in polite interest. "Miss Hume is a pretty little creature," he said. "I fancy she's sweet on that cousin of hers. It would be a suitable match."

"I suppose so." Georgy's tone was flat. "How long have you been in Town, Pam?"

"I arrived today, and lost no time in presenting myself at your door, as you see," he answered lightly. "I was hoping that perhaps you might care to drive out somewhere with me this afternoon, as the weather is fine."

"Oh, no, I'm sorry, I can't — I have an appointment with my hairdresser."

He surveyed the glowing glory of her hair.

"Does he hope to improve it?" he asked, with a quizzical smile! "Unhappy man! He has an impossible task!"

"You are a shameless flatterer!" said Georgy severely.

"No. I only speak the truth." He gave her a serious look. "You have beautiful hair, my dear Georgy."

"Oh, stuff! It's of no account in my family, you know — we all have it."

"But it is only in the females that it is so devastating," he said, significantly.

She was a shade embarrassed by his

manner. He often paid her compliments, but not usually in so serious a vein. He sensed her uneasiness, and changed the subject.

"By the way, there's an invitation to Lady Routledge's soirée among my correspondence," he said, easily. "I notice it is for this evening. Will you by any chance be going? If so, perhaps you will allow me to escort you?"

"Oh, yes, I can scarcely refuse Lady Routledge. She was such a close friend of Mama's, you know. There's to be some new Italian singer — but I fear it will be a tedious affair, when all is said! You will hardly wish to go."

"On the contrary," he replied, quietly. "I wish to go very much. It will not be tedious to me, I assure you."

17

Lady Routledge's Soirée

WHATEVER Pamyngton may have felt about Lady Routledge's soirée, Georgiana found it every bit as boring as she had expected. The Italian singer had a good voice, but she accompanied her songs by a series of affected gestures which went very ill with her gross figure. Georgy was hard put to it not to laugh. Indeed at one point, happening to catch the eye of a sixteen-year old boy who had not yet returned to school because he had just recovered from chicken-pox, she did dissolve into helpless giggles. This drew down a severe reprimand on the unlucky schoolboy; but paradoxically, the incident made him Georgy's slave for the rest of the evening.

Pamyngton was at her side whenever he could manoeuvre it, but as both of them had so many acquaintances there, this was not as often as he could have wished. On one occasion when they were separated, Georgy slipped into a vacant chair among a group towards the back of the room. The Italian singer had just embarked on yet another song and Georgy felt there was a distinct advantage in not being too near the front to watch the performance. Evidently there were others in the room who were also able to resist the delights of the entertainment offered them, for Georgy observed several people in the chairs in front of her who had their heads together in animated conversation.

Her attention was suddenly caught by the sound of her own name coming from two ladies who were sitting directly before her. She had not paid them any particular attention before, but now she studied their profiles and made the discovery that one of them was Mrs. Curshawe. As they made very little attempt to moderate their voices, she could not avoid hearing most of what they were saying. As she listened, her indignation rose.

" . . . not at all a proper way for an unmarried girl to behave, whatever privileges she may fancy birth and fortune allow her. Truth to tell, my dear Mrs. Holder, I was vastly relieved when I could bring my Caroline away from what I can only consider an undesirable influence; though naturally I'm sorry to say such a thing of Caroline's prospective sister-in-law."

"Young people today though, ma'am, have not the strict sense of decorum which you and I were taught when we were young. There is a wildness — most deplorable! I'm sure for my part I cannot understand what they would be at!" A certain relish entered the speaker's tone. "You say she was flirting abominably with every man in sight? Well, that is nothing new for *that* young lady, Mrs. Curshawe, as anyone knows who has been about a little in the world of fashion."

"No, but it was the particular manner of it, ma'am. My poor Henry — I wouldn't say this to anyone else, but I know I can rely on *your* discretion — he was quite bewitched, and I doubt if he'll recover for a long time. You know what a steady, serious-minded young man he is." Her companion nodded. "Well, she led him on to make her an offer of marriage, which, of course, she had not the slightest intention of accepting; and then she so taunted him that afterwards he almost challenged my Lord Pamyngton to a duel — though I did not know of this until after we had left Buckinghamshire."

Mrs. Holder's nose twitched with interest, but she gave a shocked exclamation.

"I rely on you, of course, dear ma'am, not to say anything of this to anyone else," went on Mrs. Curshawe.

"Oh my dear Mrs. Curshawe, I shall not breathe a syllable, you may depend! But I suppose your son would have fought Lord Pamyngton because he is the favoured suitor? The whole town predicts that he will win Georgiana Eversley in the end."

"There was more to it than that," said Mrs. Curshawe, darkly, "though I do not know the whole. You can well imagine that my Henry would not wish to talk of the affair. But that is only a part of what went on. There was some young doctor down there, who was attending Hugh Eversley's wife — she is soon to be confined you know — "

"Ah, Beau Eversley!" sighed Mrs. Holder. "Now there's a handsome man if you like! But before his marriage his amours were the talk of the town, you know, so evidently it runs in the family! But don't let me interrupt you, ma'am — you were telling me about some young man — a *doctor*, I think you said?"

"Yes, a doctor," repeated Mrs. Curshawe. "And you would have thought that someone like that, in a totally different walk of life, might have been safe from the lady's attentions. But no, such is evidently her vanity, that she must be trying to enslave every man! It seems she laid a wager with her younger brother — as wild as the rest of them I can assure you — that she would bring this poor young man to her feet before she left the country for Town."

"And did she succeed?" asked her neighbour in the tone of one who was getting rather better entertainment than she had hoped for at a mere musical evening.

"Admirably — for her purpose!" snapped Mrs. Curshawe. "But I fancy she may have been told a few home truths by the young doctor. From what I saw of him, he wasn't one to mince his words! And a good thing too, for it's high time someone took the minx down a peg or two!"

The song ended, and there was a burst of applause. As it subsided, Georgiana deliberately dropped her reticule underneath Mrs. Curshawe's chair. Then she bent forward with a mischievous smile on her face, but the flame of anger in her green eyes. She tapped the older woman on the shoulder.

"I am sorry to disturb you, ma'am," she said, politely, "but while I was sitting behind you during the last song, I dropped my reticule under your chair. Perhaps if you could move a little to one side — "

As they turned and realized who was addressing them, the look on both their faces seemed to Georgy an ample revenge for all that she had suffered from their whispered malice. Mrs. Curshawe stuttered something, and moved her chair at once. Georgy bent down to recover her property, then rose, giving them a sardonic smile.

"Careless of me, but it was soon retrieved," she said meaningly. "What a pity that a lost reputation is not so easily recovered!"

She did not stay to see the effect of this, but walked away. She had scarcely taken a step when the schoolboy was at her side.

"I say, Miss Eversley, can I get you some refreshment?" he asked shyly. "There's a famous spread in the anteroom beyond — mountains of pastries, and a great ham, and ices and jellies galore, besides I don't know how many other things! More than we see at school in a month of Sundays. I dare say you're feeling a bit hungry, I confess I am myself."

It was on the tip of Georgy's tongue to say that she was leaving, for this had been her intention. But looking into the eager yet diffident face which was only just an inch or two above the level of her own, she knew that she could not make such a churlish reply. It was not so long since her brother Freddy had been the same age as this boy. Experience and a quick perception told her that he was feeling like a fish out of water, and that only in herself had he recognized a kindred spirit. She gave him a friendly, encouraging smile.

"Why, that's prodigious kind in you! By all means let's go and sample these delights together." She placed her hand lightly on his arm, and saw the quick flush of pleasure which touched his cheek. "But I don't think I know your name," she added.

"I'm a Routledge, ma'am — one of Lady Routledge's grandsons. But you can call me Clive, if you like," he offered with the air of one conferring a jealously guarded favour.

"Then I will call you Clive, and you shall call me Georgy, for your Grandmother was a very close friend of my mother's," she replied. "Very well, Clive — lead on to the feast."

They were both laughing as they made their way to the refreshment room. On the way they passed close to Mrs. Curshawe and her gossiping friend. Georgy caught the meaning glances which the two ladies bestowed first on her and then on each other as she passed. The angry flash returned for a moment to her eyes. She guessed they would be saying that Georgiana Eversley was at her old tricks again, that even an innocent schoolboy was not safe from her. She tossed her head, and the boy at her side glanced enquiringly at her.

"What's up, Miss Georgy?" he asked in the direct way of his kind. "Have I somehow annoyed you? 'Pon my word, I wouldn't for the world! Assure you — truly!"

She laughed. "Did I look angry, then?"

He grinned in relief. "Mad as fire. There's a sort of green light comes in your eyes. But I'm glad it wasn't my doing — who was it who put you out of humour then?"

They had entered the room, and now stood before a long table loaded with food. She saw with amusement that Clive's attention began to wander from her.

"Oh, just two females whom I find repulsive," she replied airly.

"Most of 'em are — oh, not you,

of course!" he hastily amended the thoughtless statement. "But what would you like, ma'am? Look at that delicious trifle piled high with cream! And then there's the pastry — though of course ham is more filling. Perhaps we could start with that, and then work our way on to — "

"So this is where you are, Clive," said a voice at their elbows. "Your Mama has been searching for you all over."

The boy turned and saw his grandmother standing there. His eyes travelled back to the loaded table. "Does she require me at once, ma'am?" he asked wistfully. "I was just about to get something for Miss Eversley to eat."

"Yes, certainly she does. She is in the other room on the left as you enter. You need not worry about Miss Eversley, Clive," as he turned reluctantly to go. "I will see that her wants are supplied."

"And don't worry about yourself," whispered Georgy, "there'll be plenty here when you return, you may depend."

"You're a right one, Miss Georgy!" he whispered back, sketching a bow before he hurried off.

"What in the world were you two whispering about?" demanded Lady Routledge, tapping Georgiana's arm with her fan. "It comes to something, puss, when you make a conquest of a babe like that!"

Something in her guest's face told her that this little pleasantry had misfired. She changed the subject smoothly asking if Georgy would care for some refreshment.

"No thank you, ma'am. I was just about to seek you out and take my leave as a matter of fact. It has been a delightful evening, but I have had so many late nights just lately that I feel a trifle fagged. I am sure you will understand."

"Of course, my dear child." Lady Routledge studied Georgy's face thoughtfully. "It seemed to me you were not quite in spirits when you arrived. Perhaps you've been overdoing things — you young people will try to cram eight and forty hours into every day! I suppose this means that you will be depriving me of Pamyngton's company too. He was your escort this evening was he not?"

Georgy assented.

"Then I will send someone to find him. He is a dear boy, is he not? So like his Mama! Never out of humour, and always ready to oblige a hostess by helping to entertain a difficult guest — I declare I do not know any gentleman I would rather invite to my occasions. But there" — darting a shrewd glance at Georgy — "I dare say I need not sing his praises to you, of all people. Tell me, my dear — you won't mind an old friend asking you, I'm sure, for I've known you since you were a baby — tell me, do you mean to have him in the end? I'm sure you couldn't find a better husband anywhere!"

"I — I don't think of marriage at present," stammered Georgy.

"It's time you did, my dear. How old are you, now? One and twenty isn't it? At your age I had brought two children into the world — and so had your Mama. Take my advice, and don't leave marriage for too long. A woman's notions become nicer, the older she gets, until no man seems quite good enough for her, and she most likely ends up as an old maid. And that will never do for you, my dear Georgiana. You are by far too handsome and lively for such a fate." Seeing the expression on Georgy's face, she broke off and patted her hand. "There, my dear, I've said enough, even for an old friend. I won't keep you any more, but let you go home."

After Pamyngton had handed Georgy up into his carriage, he began some light-hearted comments on the evening's entertainment. He soon found that she was not attending, however, and said no more for a time. When the silence had lasted for several minutes, he asked her solicitously if she felt tired.

"No — yes — I don't know!" replied Georgy, impatiently. "It has been a stupid, boring evening!"

"Has anything happened to vex you particularly?" he asked carefully.

She was about to deny it, but changed her mind at the last minute.

"Oh, that stupid female, Mrs. Curshawe!" she answered with a shrug. "She was gossiping about me to one of her cronies, and I chanced to overhear them. They say eavesdroppers never hear any good of themselves," she added ruefully, attempting a smile.

"I am sure you need pay no attention to the idle chatter of elderly females who have no better way of passing their time," he replied.

"No — but Mrs. Curshawe was talking about her son, and — and saying that I had led him on," went on Georgy, indignantly. "And as she happens to be the third person to accuse me of that in the last few days — without the slightest justification! — I just felt — oh, I can't tell you! Mad as fire!" she concluded, borrowing from Clive Routledge's vocabulary.

He nodded. "Who were the others?"

She shrugged again, and as they passed under a street lamp, he saw that her lips were trembling.

"My brother Hugh, for one," she said, unsteadily.

"And the other?"

He thought she was not going to answer; but after a moment she said in a very thin voice, "Dr. Graham."

He drew in his breath sharply. "I see. One might ask what concern it was of his?"

Georgy's hands clenched tightly together in her lap. "He — he knows about the bet," she said. "Henry Curshawe told him."

"I see."

"No, you don't!" she said explosively, and suddenly burst into tears.

"Oh, my dear!"

He placed an arm about her shoulders, at the same time fishing a large white handkerchief from his pocket.

"Use this," he said gently, offering it to her.

She pressed the handkerchief to her face, turning slightly to lay her head on his shoulder.

"Oh, Pam!" she whimpered, incoherently. "What a fool I am!"

"Nothing of the kind," he murmured, comfortingly, stroking her hair with gentle fingers.

She sobbed quietly for a moment. He tightened his hold on her, but said nothing. Presently she took the handkerchief from her face, and looked up at him, still nestling against his shoulder.

"You're such a comfort, Pam!"

271

Her green eyes were misty with tears, her expression that of a small lost child. A swift surge of compassion caught at him. He bent his head and kissed her very gently on the lips.

"Give me the right to comfort you always, my dear," he whispered, as he drew back reluctantly from the embrance.

She smiled ruefully, shaking her head.

"Why not?" he persisted, though still gently. "Could you not learn to love me a little, Georgy? I worship you — but then, you must know that already."

"That's why it wouldn't be fair," she answered, with another shake of the head. "I don't return your feelings in the same measure. You deserve nothing less."

"Few of us are lucky enough to get our deserts," he said. "A little affection from you would mean more to me than another woman's entire devotion."

"You think so now, but it wouldn't do. You could not be content with less than everything — no one could."

He smiled. "Ah, but you are such a whole-hearted person, my love — if I may call you so." He paused, but she made no objection. "Let me be the judge of my own happiness. If you will only be my wife, I will be content to wait for your affection to grow. You see" — looking down at her tenderly — "I don't think so poorly of myself as to believe that it won't grow, given time."

Her look was thoughtful. "You may be right," she said, slowly. "I *am* very fond of you, after all, and everyone seems agreed that we are prodigiously well suited. We have had some capital fun together — and I can't imagine that you would ever vex me, or hurt me — " she broke off. "But there's no — no — magic," she concluded, sadly.

"Perhaps we can conjure some up, together," he said, hoarsely. "Georgy — my love — "

She raised her head hurriedly from his shoulder, and placed a restraining hand on his chest.

"No, you mustn't kiss me again, Pam. Not yet — not now. I want to think — "

He raised the hand to his lips. "Must you think, my darling? Marry me first, and we'll do the thinking together afterwards."

"It would be too late then." She moved a little away from him, and he released her hand, watching her face intently. "Pam" — her tone had changed to one of decision — "I know what I must do. I must make up my mind, once and for all."

"That's just what I've been trying to make you do — "

"Yes, but not now," she interrupted him, "not like this, when I am upset and looking for comfort. I must go right away from you, Pam — I must be able to think — "

He started to protest, but she cut him short.

"I shall go back to Hugh's," she said, decidedly, "and stay there until after Sue has had her baby. That means I shall be there for some weeks. And you are not to follow me, Pam, nor to write to me — "

"But that's too cruel, Georgy! What on earth shall I do with myself while you are away? But I suppose" — with a resigned sigh — "you will do whatever you choose." He turned towards her again. "Will nothing persuade you to give me an answer now?"

"No, Pam. I must be sure. But when I do return to London, I will give you my answer. And I promise you there shall be no shilly-shallying on my part — it will be plain 'Yes or No.'"

"Very well, dearest Georgiana, if you will have it so, I suppose I must be content. But it is monstrous hard."

18

Intercession

CHARACTERISTICALLY, Georgy lost no time in carrying out her intention, but posted back to Fulmer Towers on the following day. With less than a fortnight to go to her confinement Susan was very pleased to see her.

"Aunt Lavinia and Mrs. Levibond between them are nearly killing me with kindness, Georgy! I was never so cossetted in my life! It will be good to have someone near me who's able to treat me as if I were a normal female, and not something made of delicate china."

"Margaret Radley is a sensible enough woman."

"Oh, the Radleys returned to London yesterday, after Pam had left. There is only Freddy here, now, and he will be gone in a day or two."

"Well, Sue, you wouldn't wish to have

a large party in the house for your lying-in."

"I assure you I don't mind how many people there may be, just as long as you are here — and Hugh, of course. What I do feel is the need of someone lively about me."

But during the next few days, Susan was not to find her sister-in-law at all a lively companion. Georgy seemed to have developed a taste for solitary rides and walks, and for poring over books or magazines instead of indulging in the light-hearted chatter which they had always shared. Susan could not help but notice, too, that very often the book that Georgy was supposed to be reading would rest in her hands at the same page for half an hour at a stretch while her eyes gazed unseeingly at the print. Undoubtedly there was something very wrong: Susan recalled the way her sister-in-law had rushed off just over a week ago to London and felt certain that, whatever the trouble was, it had started then. She determined to get to the bottom of it, and with this in view persuaded Georgy to take a walk with her in the shrubbery one morning. Aunt Lavinia, who disliked all forms of exercise, was glad to let them go alone.

They strolled along the paths in silence for a while. They passed a couple of gardeners busy sweeping up the golden leaves and transporting them in wheelbarrows to a great mound from which fragrant blue smoke issued.

"I love the smell of garden bonfires," said Susan, breaking the silence.

"Yes," answered Georgy, absently. "But it's sad to see those beautiful leaves burnt. Still" — with a sigh — "I suppose all beauty has to fade. Autumn is a melancholy season, don't you think?"

"Not to me — not at present!" laughed Susan.

"No, I forgot. Of course, you are happy, so you will not feel it."

"And aren't you happy, Georgy?"

The other girl shrugged. "I don't know — no, I don't think so. Not particularly — "

"Be honest, love, and admit it," urged Susan, gently. "Something has made you unhappy. I know it — you cannot take me in. I know you too well."

"I suppose you do."

Susan waited a moment for something to be added to this grudging admission. When her sister-in-law still kept silent, she prompted, "Well, then — don't you intend to tell me what it is?"

Georgy kicked at a stone lying in the path in a way that either Mrs. Curshawe or Aunt Lavinia would have unhesitatingly condemned as unladylike.

"I'm not sure that I can," she muttered. "I'm not sure that I know myself, altogether."

"Well, I think it would help you to talk about it," said Susan, firmly. "I've been watching you since you came back, Georgy, and you've been behaving just like a broody hen! All those books you pretend to read — and you're always slipping off on your own on one pretext or another — it doesn't require anyone with a very intimate knowledge of your character to see that you are not at all yourself at present."

Georgy gave a short laugh. "I suppose I have been rather a surly creature. Poor Sue, you deserve better of me! I am supposed to be keeping your spirits up."

"My spirits were never better, but we really must try to see what can be done to mend yours. Won't you trust me, love? We always used to confide in each other, once."

The faint reproach stirred Georgy's conscience.

"I know, my dear, but it would be brutal of me to burden you with my troubles at present. You must see that. Besides, there is nothing so very dreadful, after all," she added, with an attempt at lightness which did not quite succeed.

"Then tell me, if it isn't so very dreadful, why has it changed you from a lively, carefree girl into a dreary, brooding female?"

"Oh, dear, is it as bad as that?" asked Georgy, with a laugh. "Very well, Sue, I'll tell you. Since I came back here, I have been trying to make up my mind whether or not to accept an offer of marriage."

"An offer — accept?" squeaked Susan, in delight, seizing her sister-in-law's arm excitedly. "Georgy, my love — who? Who is it? Tell me at once!"

"You'd best not get too excited, Sue,

in your state of health," Georgy warned her. "It's Pam. He asked me to marry him, the day he returned to Town."

"Oh, but you'll have him!" declared Susan. "Pam! No one could be more suitable — there could be no man I'd rather see you marry!"

"So everyone says," agreed Georgy, doubtfully.

"But you're not sure? And that is what worries you so?"

Georgy nodded. "I came here to think it out. At least, I was coming anyway, because I'd promised you; and it seemed a good opportunity. I asked Pam not to follow me here, and I'm to give him my answer when I return to Town."

"Absence makes the heart grow fonder, they say."

"Oh, *fond*!" scoffed Georgy. "Yes, I am fond enough of Pam, Sue — but is that sufficient? Is it a sure foundation for marriage?"

"Many have less," Susan reminded her. "Had your father seen fit to arrange a match for you as others have done before now, you might have found yourself tied to someone you could barely tolerate."

"But such is not the case. Papa would never force me into a marriage, whatever fathers of other unlucky females may do. His thought is all for my happiness, and I know he will allow me to choose for myself — be it who it may. All I need to consider is what I want."

"You always could twist your father around your little finger," said Susan, with a smile. "And no doubt if you accept Pam — which I hope you will — you'll bring him into the same happy state of subjection, too. Sometimes I wonder if you do not need a man who will be your master, instead — "

She broke off, frowning thoughtfully.

"Oh, well, don't let's worry about me," said Georgy, hurriedly. "Susan, you aren't walking too far, are you? Perhaps we'd better return to the house now."

"No, I'm all right, though I think we will turn towards the house, as I expect the doctor to pay me a visit some time this morning."

"I thought you said he called yesterday," replied Georgy, trying to keep her voice casual.

"So he did. But he said then that my baby might arrive sooner than we had expected, so he would call every day just in case."

"You didn't tell me that," Georgy accused.

"I did, my dear, but you were not attending. Indeed, I am surprised that you are even able to recall my mentioning his visit."

"Oh, I'm sorry, Sue! Forgive me, but you know the reason. I imagine, tho'," she added, gazing intently at the ground, "you will be anxious to see Dr. Hume's return to the village."

Susan stopped abruptly, and stared. "Now I know your wits have been wool-gathering!" she declared. "Dr. Hume has returned, and came to see me yesterday. I told you that, along with the rest."

Georgy looked up quickly. "He has? Then I suppose — " she hesitated, and a slight flush coloured her cheeks — "I expect — most likely his nephew has already gone back to London?"

They had both halted now and stood facing each other. As Susan studied the flushed, unhappy face before her, she came to an almost incredible conclusion.

"Dr. Graham leaves his uncle's house tomorrow," she answered, quietly. "He came with Dr. Hume yesterday to pay his respects and take leave of us all, but you were out riding at the time."

"Then I shan't see him again." The words came out slowly, as though travelling a long distance. "Perhaps it is best. We always," she added in a brisker tone, with an attempt at liveliness, "quarrel whenever we meet. Come along, Sue! We've been out here quite long enough, I am sure, and talking so seriously, too. It's enough to give you the vapours!"

She drew Susan's arm through hers, and steered her purposefully towards the house, keeping up a laughing flow of trivialities until they had crossed the threshold.

But Susan was not deceived: Having penetrated Georgy's guard during that revealing moment in the garden, she could now understand the moody silences which had afflicted the other girl ever since her return. She wondered if Georgy really understood herself. Whether she did or not, the decision she was trying to reach would prove just as difficult and painful in the making. Susan wanted desperately to help, but could see no way of doing so. Perhaps it was better to leave matters as they stood, and hope that Georgy would decide to marry Pam. Pam would take care of her. It was easy to see that he adored Georgy. So much adoration could scarcely fail to draw forth an answering love. She kept revolving variations of these comforting thoughts in her mind for the rest of the morning. Dr. Hume came and went, repeating that she might expect to be confined any day now, and Hugh looked into her boudoir to find her sitting lost in thought.

"What, you, too, my dearest?" he teased her, gently. "Isn't it enough for my sister to sit brooding around the house, without passing the habit on to my wife."

He dropped a kiss on her brow, and demanded the latest medical report. Susan told him, and for a while they sat side by side and hand in hand, talking quietly of domestic affairs. Presently Susan changed the subject abruptly.

"Hugh, dearest, do you really think Georgy should marry Pam?"

"How you do dot about, my love — just like a butterfly," he replied, smiling at her. "Why, yes — Pam. Certainly. An excellent match. Why? Have you any doubts? You need not concern yourself, though — Georgy will do exactly what she pleases in the matter of marriage."

"But you think he would be the best person for her?" insisted Susan.

"No, I didn't say that. I think the best person for her would be a husband who would beat her regularly, and make her pay some heed to him. But there's no likelihood of her finding anyone of the kind, and so Pam will do very well. A good chap, Pam."

"Since she returned to us she's been trying to decide whether to have him or not. She's to give him her answer when she goes back to London."

"So that's why she's been walking around with a Friday face!" said Hugh, with a laugh. "It seems my sister values her freedom more jealously than most men I know."

"I don't think," said Susan, slowly, "that it's altogether the thought of sacrificing her freedom."

"What else should hinder her?"

"I don't believe, Hugh, that she is in love with Pam."

He shrugged. "I sometimes wonder if Georgy will ever be in love with anyone. She is still a regular tomboy at bottom, you know."

"Yes, dearest. But you are wrong — I'm sure you're wrong, at least — when you say she can never be in love with anyone. It's my belief that she has fallen in love, and that's why she can't bring herself to accept Pam's proposal."

He studied her thoughtfully for a moment. "You know her better than most," he said, at last. "Who is the man? Do you know that?"

"I am only hazarding a guess," replied Susan, doubtfully. "She has not confided in me."

He put his arm round her, and smiled encouragingly down into her eyes. "Womanly intuition, eh? Come, let me hear it, my love."

"Well, then," said Susan, more confidently. "I think she's in love with George's friend, Dr. Graham."

"The devil you do!"

"Is it so very bad?" asked Susan. "Wouldn't it do?"

He was silent for a moment. "You must see there are certain difficulties," he said, at last.

She nodded. "I know. It would be an unequal match. But dear, you can't have forgotten that once you, too, contemplated marrying beneath you."

He raised her hand to his lips. "There is a certain difference," he said. "A woman takes her husband's station in society, whatever that may be, when she marries. But Graham, though he has connections of some standing, has very little himself, at present."

"But if they truly love each other, Hugh?" she asked, wistfully.

He frowned. "We can't know that. Certainly, I have noticed a marked partiality on his side, and you, who know Georgy better than most, are confident of her feelings. But even so, granted a true affection on both sides, who can say if it would survive an unequal marriage? No, she will be safer with Pam. They may never know the heady delights of love, but at least they will be spared disillusion."

"Oh, Hugh!" To his dismay, he saw there were tears in her eyes. "Have you found disillusion, then?"

"My heart's darling," he murmured, taking her face gently in his hands, and kissing her lips. "You know very well that you have made me the happiest man on earth."

"Then you won't deny Georgy her chance of a happiness such as ours, will you?" she pleaded. "If she should in some way learn the truth about her feelings — and if she and Dr. Graham should reach a point when they need someone to plead their cause to your father — "

"You are asking me to intercede for them, if necessary?"

She nodded.

"Well, my love, I don't really suppose that it ever will be necessary. He is a man of honour, and therefore unlikely to press his suit, however strong his feelings may be. He will fully appreciate that he has little to offer at present. And unless he speaks, you know, Georgy must be silent. So — "

"Do you really suppose that Georgy would be silent, if she once knew her heart? No, Hugh, you must know her better than that!"

"Hm." He pursed his lips thoughtfully. "Then perhaps it might be better if she never does understand her feelings — that is, if you are not mistaken in your reading of them."

"I am not mistaken," replied Susan, confidently. "And she will be bound to discover it sooner or later. Only suppose, Hugh, if it should be after she has wed Pam! That must not happen — she cannot marry one man while she is in love with another — it would ruin all their lives!"

"What do you expect me to do about it, my darling? Tell Graham that he must marry my sister?" asked Beau Eversley, with gentle mockery.

She shook her head unhappily. "No — for there is a misunderstanding between them — "

"A misunderstanding?" repeated her husband, dryly. "I had no notion of there being any kind of an understanding between them."

"I do not know the whole," replied Susan, hurriedly, "but Georgy did tell me that she had played off one of her jokes upon him, and that Dr. Graham was very vexed and — and disgusted with her, and not likely to — to — think well of her ever again."

"Dear me!" drawled Beau Eversley. "It certainly does sound very much like a lovers' quarrel. Has he declared himself, then? Did she tell you that?"

Susan shook her head. "No. I really *know* very little. It is just that I guess a great deal. And, Hugh, dearest" — she laid her hand on the sleeve of his coat — "I would so like to be able to help! After all, Georgy helped me, when I was so unhappy — you remember?"

"I remember, my sweeting. But in general such affairs are best left to the parties concerned. Georgy must make up her own mind — hers is a decided character, so she will not be long about the business." He glanced at her face, and saw the doubt that clouded her eyes. "Come, love, you mustn't vex yourself with gloomy thoughts at present! I promise you that if by any chance these two unlikely people should decide to wed, I will plead their cause to my father. There, now! Will that satisfy you?"

"Oh, Hugh, yes! You are so good!"

She nestled close to him.

"And now you may put the whole thing out of your head," he said, stroking her dark hair.

She nodded; but in the recesses of her mind, a plan was stirring.

19

Susan Takes A Risk

JOHN GRAHAM was packing. He would leave his uncle's house tomorrow for London, to continue his work at St. George's Hospital until the time came for him to go back to his native Edinburgh. He would not be sorry to leave Buckinghamshire. The medical experience had been useful, of course: a country practice offered a surprising variety of cases, as he had admitted yesterday to his uncle, perhaps to the older man's amusement. But at present the place affected his spirits much as a coarse bandage might chafe an open wound. Every scene served to remind him of incidents he would rather forget. The calls at Fulmer Towers, culminating in yesterday's farewell visit, had been particularly trying.

He had not seen Georgiana Eversley yesterday, although he knew that she had returned from London. Not until the visit was over did he realize how much he had wanted to see her again. There was no sense in that, he told himself angrily. Their parting had been final; nothing more remained to be said. She had tricked him finely for no better reason than her own idle amusement. She deserved every harsh reproach he had hurled at her. It only remained now to forget her.

What a pity that painful memories could not be cut out from a man's mind as harmful growths could be removed from his body. But it would not be long, he told himself, before he had mastered this weakness. His Scottish pride demanded it. A man whose ancestors had successfully repelled so many Sassenach raids on their property ought to know how to defend himself, even against a more insidious form of attack from the same source. He smiled grimly as he made the little jest to himself: at least, he had not lost his sense of humour.

The house seemed very quiet. His aunt and Mrs. Chiltern had gone to the weekly market in Amersham, and Dr. Hume had been called away to a case. Anne was still in London; she was to remain there for a month at least. His thoughts lingered uneasily for a moment on Anne. He was not unaware of the hopes entertained by Dr. and Mrs. Hume. He knew that if he chose to seek his cousin's hand in marriage, they would raise no obstacle. He was far from being conceited, but he had a strong suspicion that Anne shared their views, a suspicion brought into being by many little incidents during the time they had spent together under the same roof. He could only hope now that his cousin's feelings for him did not go too deep. He had suffered lately himself, and would not wish that particular form of pain on any human being, least of all on someone for whom he felt a genuine, though brotherly, affection. But she was young, after all, he told himself, and he was practically the first man she had ever known very well. There would be others; perhaps even now in London she was meeting some dashing Beau who would soon make her forget a young Scots doctor with nothing in particular to recommend him, and who was of no account in the world.

He straightened up from his packing on this thought, and squared his shoulders, a determined look in his dark eyes. Yes, he was of no account in the world — yet. But he would be. There would come a time when his name would be known in his chosen field of work, at any rate. And when that day came, he thought triumphantly, he would be a fitting mate even for such as Georgiana Eversley.

Damn the woman! There she was again, creeping into his thoughts. Thank goodness he was going back to London tomorrow; it should be easier there to put her out of his mind.

He heard the sound of a vehicle drawing up outside the house, and thought that it must be the gig returning. He frowned; on second thoughts, it did not sound like the gig. He went over to the window, drew aside the white dimity curtains and peered through the pane. His frown deepened. It was not the gig, but a carriage with the Eversley crest on its panels.

His heart gave a leap. Could it possibly be . . . ?

Someone was being helped from the carriage. Without pausing long enough to see who it might be, he raced from the room and went headlong down the stairs just as the knocker sounded throughout the silent house.

There was only one servant at present in the house, a little kitchenmaid of tender years, who had been dozing before the kitchen fire. She came dashing out at the summons, straightening her cap as she ran, and almost collided with Graham in the hall.

"Don't bother," he said, dismissively. "I believe it's a visitor for me."

She bobbed awkwardly, and returned to her warm seat by the fire.

Graham flung open the door, a tell-tale eagerness lighting his face. The next moment, the glow left his expression.

It was not Georgiana who stood on the threshold, but Susan Eversley. She turned to give some directions to the groom who had escorted her to the door, thus giving Graham a chance to master his feelings. The groom returned to join the coachman on the box, and the carriage moved off down the village street. When Susan turned towards him, Graham was able to greet her calmly enough, although his tone was puzzled.

"Mrs. Eversley! What can bring you here, ma'am? Pray come inside."

He put out a hand to steady her, and, closing the street door, guided her into the parlour. "I collect you have come to see my uncle. I am sorry, he is not at home at present, but I expect him back shortly. Won't you sit down? I think this chair will be comfortable for you, ma'am."

He waited until she had settled herself. Then he continued with a shade of reproach: "You ought not to have come, you know, Mrs. Eversley, and especially not without your woman in attendance. You are too near your time to be jolting about the roads in this way. I wonder you did not send for my uncle to wait on you instead."

"But it is not Dr. Hume I wish to see," replied Susan, with a smile.

He stared at her. "Not my uncle? Then who — ?"

"Yourself," she replied simply.

"I?" His tone was incredulous. "But, ma'am, I saw you yesterday — surely, if there had been anything — "

"That was no use — how could I talk to you with so many people present? And if I had sent for you today, it would have been just the same. My only dependence on being private with you was in coming here. I managed to slip out without anyone at home knowing," she went on, with an impish grin that made her look more like a schoolgirl than the wife of an acknowledged leader of fashion. "They think I am resting in my room."

He laughed, infected by her childlike glee. "Well, ma'am, it seems you tricked them nicely. But it really wasn't wise, you know it wasn't. Now that you are here, however, tell me how I can have the honour of serving you?"

For the first time, she showed some hesitation. "I want to talk to you — "

He spread his hands in an expressive gesture. "Well, here I am! Talk on, Mrs. Eversley, and welcome."

She shook her head. "It may not be so

welcome." There was another pause. "I want to talk to you about — about my sister-in-law, Georgy."

His face changed. "I don't quite see — "

She clenched her hands across the bundle that was so soon to take its place in the world as a personality. He saw her tenseness, and reminded himself to go gently with her.

"No, not that," he said quietly, unclenching her hands. "Just relax — so — there, that is better. Now — " he sat down in a chair close to hers. "What do you wish to say to me concerning Miss Eversley?"

"Only this — do you love her?"

He stared at her in amazement. She reddened under his gaze, and the pace of her breathing quickened.

"That is a very personal question," he answered gravely.

"Oh, I know it! And no doubt you think it impertinent in me to ask it — and so it is, I suppose, though I do not intend it so," said Susan, in a rush. "But I must know the answer — *I must know*," she repeated, with an energy that made her breathing more difficult. "Please tell me — truly, honestly — and don't refuse me, for I mean only the best for both of you. And there isn't much time for me," she added suddenly, a look of awareness on her face. "There isn't much time — "

He jumped to his feet. "Mrs. Eversley — "

"No, I am all right." She waved him away. "But soon, I think . . . And you must answer me, please. I must do what I came here to do, first — help me — please — "

She was in no state to be trifled with: he could not deny her.

"I will try." His eyes met hers candidly. "But I'm not sure why you ask me this. That might make a difference to my answer."

"And I can't tell you the reason until I have your answer," she replied, with some difficulty. "You must trust me, I think, will you not do so?"

"Don't distress yourself, ma'am." He leaned over and patted her hands reassuringly. "Yes, I will trust you, for I believe I may. Here is your answer, then. I do have the misfortune to be in love with Miss Eversley, but I mean to get the better of it in time. Does that satisfy you?"

She let loose a great sigh. "Ah! Now I may tell you why I wished to know. It is because *she* loves *you*. And she is trying to get the better of her feelings, too. Don't you think it would be more sensible if you both gave in, and decided to confess your affection and make the best of it by marrying?"

A surge of hope swept over him at her words, but he quenched it. "You're mistaken," he said bitterly. "I thought she was, too, once; but then I discovered that she was only taking me in — and for a wager!"

"She was taking herself in, more than you," stated Susan, firmly. "It may have started as a hoax, but I can assure you — and no one knows Georgy as I do — that it finished in good earnest! Poor dear, she is so unhappy — and all for nothing, if you say you truly care for her as she does for you. You are both very stupid — but then, people in love so often are. I was myself."

He stared at her without speaking for a moment, lost in the tumult of his thoughts. "Are you sure of this?" he asked, at last. "Has she confided in you?"

"No. But you needn't fear for that" — as she saw him shake his head — "I know Georgy, right enough, and I also know what it's like" — she smiled reminiscently — "to be in love. Hers is a clear case. The symptons are very bad, doctor. You must do something about it."

"But she hasn't actually said anything," he mused. "And you could be mistaken — there are so many obstacles in the way, even if it were true that she cares for me. I must be certain."

"Oh, then I have done with you!" exclaimed Susan in disgust. "If you won't believe me — and who should know her better than I? — then you'd best leave matters be, and let her marry Lord Pamyngton, after all!"

"Marry Pamyngton?"

"Yes, for that is what she's trying to force herself into doing at this very moment. She's to give him her answer when she returns to Town."

"By God, she shan't!" The light of battle was in his eyes. "Not unless and until she can tell me herself that she prefers him to me!"

"That's better!" remarked Susan, in a satisfied tone. She began to struggle out of the chair. "Then come back with me in the carriage, and have things out with her now. I told my coachman to be at your door in half an hour — oh!"

She ended on a long drawn out gasp. Graham moved quickly to her side. She attempted a smile, then groaned again.

"There wasn't much time — but I managed — " she panted. "I think, sir, you'll have to deliver my baby — we can't wait for Dr. Hume."

20

An Heir For Beau Eversley

AFTER Susan had gone to lie down in her room, Georgy took a horse from the stable and went riding. Her chaotic thoughts would not allow her either to be in company with others, or to stay still. She told herself that she could no longer continue in this state of indecision; something must be settled this very afternoon, or she would go out of her mind.

As she rode over deserted woodland paths thick in fallen leaves, she made a desperate attempt to set her thoughts in order. The news that John Graham was to leave his uncle's house tomorrow had come as a severe shock. She asked herself impatiently what possible difference his going could make to her. They had parted for ever in such disgust on his side that no reconciliation was possible. He must have learnt that she was now back at Fulmer Towers, and he could have found some opportunity to see her again had he wished to do so. At the very least, he could have written her a note. No, it was quite plain that he had not relented; she did not think he ever would. All his love for her had vanished, swept away by the bitterness that had engulfed him when he had learnt of her duplicity. Now he held her in contempt: she had to admit that she deserved it.

Oh, what did it matter? Why must she vex herself with thoughts of this man? It had only been a jest, trying to make him fall in love with her, and she had succeeded, had she not? He had fallen in love with her, she had won her wager — though she had never claimed payment of it from Freddy — and now the whole stupid episode could be forgotten.

But it would not be forgotten. During these past days, when she had been trying to make up her mind what her answer to Pam would be, thoughts of her last meeting with John Graham had kept obtruding themselves, clouding the issue.

A squirrel ran suddenly across her path and streaked effortlessly up the trunk of an elm, shaking down some leaves. Her horse shied slightly, recalling her to her present surroundings. She slowed the animal to a walk, and looked about her. The wood was alive with colour. Red, gold and amber leaves were thickly strewn upon the ground; the sunlight glinted along the silvery trunks of a clump of birches which stretched graceful fingers towards a sky of palest blue. She caught her breath. The beauty of nature always had the power to bring almost a physical ache to her heart; today she felt this all the more strongly because it was in similar surroundings that she and John Graham had quarrelled and parted. As though some unseen hand touched the strings of a delicate musical instrument, a vibrant melancholy filled her senses. In that moment she realized that she loved him, that he was the only man in the world for her, come what may.

She had never admitted it to herself before now. When he had taken her in his arms at their last meeting, she had responded to him with all the ardour of her impulsive nature; but after their quarrel, she had persuaded herself that it had only been a passing infatuation. She knew that hers was a volatile temperament, and had never doubted that she would forget Dr. Graham as quickly as she had yielded to his attraction.

But it had not proved so easy. Even in the hurlyburly of London, thoughts of him had kept creeping in; but here in the country, where so many scenes brought him to mind, she had not been able to think of anyone or anything else. She had come here with the intention of thinking about Pamyngton and his love for her; and all her time had been given over instead to vain regrets about the man who held her in contempt.

Only now did the true significance of this contrariness dawn on her. The magic that was missing from her affection for Pam was present in every slightest thought she had of the other man. Now that at last she had come to her senses, what was to be done?

She reined-in the horse and dismounted, to sit upon a fallen tree that lay beside the path. She must be still for a few moments and think this out. Her fingers idly dabbled in the leaves at her feet as she sat motionless, concentrating on her problem.

One thing was certain; she could never marry Pam now. If she could not have Jock Graham, she wanted no one. In that case, she thought with a little smile, it looked as though she would have to become an old maid like Aunt Lavinia, dividing her time and energies between visits to relatives and playing Lady Bountiful to the parish. She wrinkled her nose. Pooh! The part would not fit her at all. But what else was there for her to do? Dr. Graham evidently meant to take no action to heal the breach between them. No doubt his confounded Scottish pride forbade such weakness. A wave of tenderness swept over her as she recalled all the many things that endeared him to her — his strength and his weakness.

A sudden fierce possessiveness took hold of her. He was her man, now, and she decided she would not let him go without a fight. No maidenly scruples would stand in her way. She would go to him, tell him that she loved him; if he could still reject her after that — well, then indeed there was an end of it all.

She jumped up, impatiently shaking the leaves from her skirt and remounting the horse. Turning its head in the direction of the village she urged it into a gallop. Before long, she was standing in front of Dr. Hume's door. Her legs felt curiously weak, and her hand shook slightly as she raised the knocker. She set her lips firmly, and waited in some inward trepidation.

She waited a long time — so long, that she began to think there could be no one at home. She felt a flood of relief for a moment, but it was quickly followed by disappointment. After screwing up her courage to come here, she would have preferred to get the matter over.

She was about to turn away when the door opened a few inches, and a small head in a mop cap that was slightly askew peered round it.

"Yes'm?"

"Is Dr. Graham at home?" Georgy's voice sounded strange even to her own ears.

The head nodded vigorously. "Yes'm

— but he's busy — "

"Perhaps I could wait somewhere indoors until the doctor is disengaged?"

The owner of the head looked doubtful, but she opened the door and allowed Georgy to enter.

"I'll tell Dr. Graham, 'm," she mumbled, opening the door into the parlour.

Georgy stepped inside the room, leaving the door ajar. She could not sit down, but remained standing with her eyes fixed on the door. Minutes that seemed like years dragged by as she waited. She felt her courage ebbing away with every second that passed. In another moment, she would have fled, but at last a quick footstep sounded outside the room. The door was pushed wide, and Graham entered.

For a moment, they both stared at each other. Georgy all at once became conscious of her appearance, and put up her hands to try and straighten her windblown hair. She realized that leaves and bits of twig were clinging here and there to her riding dress, and found herself wishing fervently that he could have seen her looking her best, instead of for all the world like a raggle-taggle gypsy. And then she saw that he, too, was looking a trifle dishevelled, without a coat and with his shirt sleeves rolled up above the elbow. She had never seen him so before.

"You!"

He broke the silence with the one word, spoken in a tone which she found difficult to interpret. She feared it might be disgust, and the thought revived her flagging courage.

"Yes. Me . . . " She spoke quietly, but earnestly. "Listen — I've got to talk to you, Jock . . . You would not hear me before — now you *must*."

"I will hear you," he replied gently. "But not now — there's no time." The pace of his words quickened. "Your sister-in-law is here, and about to give birth to her child." Georgy gave a startled exclamation. "She came here alone, and there's no one in the house at present except the little maid you saw, who's too young to be of use. I need someone to assist me — will you do it?"

Fresh air and exercise had whipped

the colour into Georgy's face, but now it paled noticeably. She stepped back a pace.

"I? Help? But — but — " she stammered, "I don't know if I could. I've no notion — I've never — I don't think — "

He took a quick step forward and grasped her wrist. "You could — and you will!" His tone was firm. "There's no one else. I've sent the coach back for Mrs. Levibond, but the odds are she won't arrive in time. You are woman enough to help another woman in her time of need, I know you are. And you owe something to Mrs. Eversley — she came here to do you a service, at some risk to herself. Come, now — "

She still hesitated. He gave an appealing tug at her arm; then he released it and turned towards the door.

"I must go to my patient," he said, in a tone deep of disappointment. "I'm sorry — perhaps I ask too much, even for one of your courage — "

"No, wait!" She moved forward to his side. Her face was pale and serious, but he saw by the determination there that he could rely on her to do whatever was necessary without betraying any further weakness. "I'm ready — only tell me what I must do."

It was about an hour later that the Eversley coach drew up again outside Dr. Hume's house, with a stamping of hoofs and jingling of harness. From its interior leapt Hugh Eversley, looking something less than his usual imperturbable self, and a flustered Mrs. Levibond, with the strings of her bonnet untied and a cloak flung heedlessly about her shoulders.

They were admitted almost at once, and invited to take a seat in the parlour. Beau Eversley swept the offer impatiently aside.

"Take me to Mrs. Eversley," he commanded the little maid.

She had just begun a reply when he heard a door opening on the other side of the hall. He twisted round on his heel quickly.

Georgiana was standing there, a bundle in her arms.

He was at her side in a stride. She held the bundle up, gently pulling aside the shawl which covered it, Hugh gazed into an unbelievably tiny face, wrinkled like a very old man's and crowned with a thick crop of the Eversley hair.

"A son for you, Hugh," she said quietly. "Congratulations!"

He touched the little cheek with a tentative finger. The small mouth opened, and a thin wail emerged. At that sound, Mrs. Levibond rushed forward with arms outstretched.

"Give him to me, Miss Georgy!" she commanded, taking the baby to her ample bosom. "The sweet lamb!" she crooned, bending over the child, who was now giving tongue with surprising gusto for one so young. "The little sweeting, then!"

"Susan?" asked Hugh, in an almost pleading tone. "Take me to her, Georgy!"

Georgy nodded, and pushed open the surgery door. Dr. Graham was standing just inside it, evidently about to emerge. He answered Hugh's unspoken question at once.

"Your wife is very well, sir. Tired, of course, but that will pass. Everything was most satisfactory — a healthy infant, male. But no doubt you'll have heard

315

already. You may see her for a little while now, but afterwards she'll need some sleep."

Hugh seized his hand in a firm clasp. "Bless you, my dear fellow," he said, with more emotion in his voice than Georgy could ever remember hearing. Then he went quickly but quietly into the room, closing the door softly.

Graham took Georgy's hands in his, and looked into her eyes, which were swimming in tears.

"You were splendid," he said quietly, "but then I knew you would be. And now," he went on, in a brisker tone, "I think what we all need is a good strong dish of tea."

He released her and went in search of the housemaid.

They were all three sitting in the parlour drinking tea when Dr. Hume returned, followed in a short time by his wife and the housekeeper. If Dr. Hume felt any disappointment at having lost the privilege of bringing a future Viscount Eversley into the world, he managed to conceal it admirably. He took a look at both mother and child, congratulated

Beau Eversley on the state of their health, and Dr. Graham on having conducted a successful delivery.

"You should congratulate Miss Eversley, too, uncle," said Graham. "Her help was invaluable."

There was a little pause before Dr. Hume found the right answer to make to this remark. Mrs. Hume considered Georgiana thoughtfully out of the corner of her eye. She was not *quite* sure that she altogether approved of the part Miss Eversley had played. To be sure, it had been awkward for John with no other female in the house at the time — but still, a gently reared girl such as Georgiana Eversley to be acting as a midwife! Such things were not thought of — she would not have cared for Anne to do the office, even though she had been reared in a medical family. Still, in her position Miss Eversley could perhaps afford to be a law unto herself; and there was no denying that she was a good-hearted, generous young lady, and a brave one, too.

"Indeed I do," Dr. Hume was saying, with a smile. "It was fortunate that Miss

317

Eversley chanced to be here."

"Yes, why were you here, Georgy?" asked Hugh, who was now more or less restored to his normally observant frame of mind. "Did you accompany Susan? I still don't know why she came here."

"She'll tell you herself later on," replied Georgy, a slight flush coming to cheeks which Graham noticed were still a little paler than usual. "I think she'd prefer to explain."

Hugh nodded, tacitly agreeing to let the subject lie for the present, and turned the conversation instead to arrangements for the nursing of Susan and the baby until such time as they could safely be moved to Fulmer Towers. In the midst of all the talk, Georgy felt Graham's eye upon her. She looked across at him, and saw that he was pleading with her to step outside the room.

She gave a brief nod, and watched him slip quietly away. No one commented on his absence, so after a few moments she rose and followed him.

He was waiting in the hall, and guided her without speaking into a small, book-lined room. It was now getting dusk, but he did not light the candles. They stood before the fireplace, where the bright glow of the red coals lit their faces.

"She told me that you love me," stated Graham, simply. "Is that the truth?"

Georgy nodded, not yet able to speak.

"I thought you did, at first, when you allowed me to embrace you in the gardens, that time — but when I learnt about the wager, it seemed to me that you must have been play-acting. I was mad — fighting mad — and in no mood to listen to reason. Besides, it seemed against all reason, when I came to consider it, that you could really care for me."

"I'm — I'm sorry," she said, in a low tone. "I do understand how you must have felt. Only, of course, after that I was certain that all your affection for me must be dead — and I was too proud to let you suspect that my own feelings had been genuine, all the time — "

"*All* the time?" he queried, with an ironical smile.

"We-ell . . . "

"When was it? When did you find that you cared for me in earnest, after all?"

"Oh — that's hard to say." She considered for a moment. "No, perhaps it isn't. I think it was at the ball — when you came to ask me to dance, and I was engaged — do you remember?"

"I remember very well." His voice dropped to a whisper, and he took her hands. "It was the moment just before that when I fell in love with you — when I looked across the room at you. I can't explain, but everything seemed changed in that moment — "

She nodded, smiling up into his eyes. "Yes, it was then," she said, softly, "but I didn't realize it at the time. Only when you — when we met in the gardens that day."

"You mean when I kissed you — like this?"

Some time later, they drew apart, though he still kept his arm about her.

"So you'll marry me?" he asked.

She nodded shyly.

"What about your family? They won't like it."

She shrugged. "They'll come round. Papa is always indulgent towards me, and anyway I am of an age to please myself. Besides Hugh will be on our side now. After what you've done for him today, he would most likely give you half his fortune if you desired it, let alone a troublesome sister."

"I don't desire his fortune, or anyone's. What I achieve will be by my own efforts — with you helping me." He looked down at her hair glowing in the firelight, and his eyes filled with tenderness. "We shall do wonders together, my love. Though I dare say," he added, with a whimsical desire to lend a touch of lightness to his words, "that we may quarrel now and then."

"I expect we shall," replied Georgy, with an arch look. "You can be a prodigious bully at times!"

"And you can be a headstrong minx," he retorted, stroking her hair. "I wonder what the good people of Edinburgh will make of you?"

"Pooh, Edinburgh!" she scoffed, teasing him. "'Tis but an ignorant Scottish township, after all!"

"It's a beautiful city, Georgy, and I know you will come to love it as I do. The old castle up there, dominating the other buildings, is a sight to stir the imagination — "

" . . . of any Scot," she finished for him, with a light laugh. "But I won't tease you, dearest. I promise to admire your town as much as even you could wish. Oh, and Jock!" she finished, excitedly. "I have a wonderful notion! Why do we not go to Scotland to be married? We could run away to Gretna Green — it would be most romantic!"

He laughed and drew her to him again. "My wild bride," he said in gentle mockery. "It's an attractive scheme, but I shan't allow you to persuade me to it. Our wedding will be the talk of both capitals, as it is. Not but what," he added, with a frown, "a runaway wedding wouldn't be preferable to me to one of those dreadful London affairs with all the fashionable world present. I won't do that, Georgy, and so I warn you. We'll be wed quietly, here in the village church, as soon as may be."

"Whatever you say, my love," said Georgy, demurely, "the village church will do as well as any other, for my part. But as to *quietly*," she continued, a gleam of mischief in her green eyes, "why, I'll wager — "

He put his finger on her lips. "No more wagers," he said, softly, bending his face to hers.

THE END

THE WILDERNESS WALK
Sheila Bishop

Stifling unpleasant memories of a misbegotten romance in Cleave with Lord Francis Aubrey, Lavinia goes on holiday there with her sister. The two women are thrust into a romantic intrigue involving none other than Lord Francis.

THE RELUCTANT GUEST
Rosalind Brett

Ann Calvert went to spend a month on a South African farm with Theo Borland and his sister. They both proved to be different from her first idea of them, and there was Storr Peterson — the most disturbing man she had ever met.

ONE ENCHANTED SUMMER
Anne Tedlock Brooks

A tale of mystery and romance and a girl who found both during one enchanted summer.

CLOUD OVER MALVERTON
Nancy Buckingham

Dulcie soon realises that something is seriously wrong at Malverton, and when violence strikes she is horrified to find herself under suspicion of murder.

AFTER THOUGHTS
Max Bygraves

The Cockney entertainer tells stories of his East End childhood, of his RAF days, and his post-war showbusiness successes and friendships with fellow comedians.

MOONLIGHT
AND MARCH ROSES
D. Y. Cameron

Lynn's search to trace a missing girl takes her to Spain, where she meets Clive Hendon. While untangling the situation, she untangles her emotions and decides on her own future.

NURSE ALICE IN LOVE
Theresa Charles

Accepting the post of nurse to little Fernie Sherrod, Alice Everton could not guess at the romance, suspense and danger which lay ahead at the Sherrod's isolated estate.

POIROT INVESTIGATES
Agatha Christie

Two things bind these eleven stories together — the brilliance and uncanny skill of the diminutive Belgian detective, and the stupidity of his Watson-like partner, Captain Hastings.

LET LOOSE THE TIGERS
Josephine Cox

Queenie promised to find the long-lost son of the frail, elderly murderess, Hannah Jason. But her enquiries threatened to unlock the cage where crucial secrets had long been held captive.

THE TWILIGHT MAN
Frank Gruber

Jim Rand lives alone in the California desert awaiting death. Into his hermit existence comes a teenage girl who blows both his past and his brief future wide open.

DOG IN THE DARK
Gerald Hammond

Jim Cunningham breeds and trains gun dogs, and his antagonism towards the devotees of show spaniels earns him many enemies. So when one of them is found murdered, the police are on his doorstep within hours.

THE RED KNIGHT
Geoffrey Moxon

When he finds himself a pawn on the chessboard of international espionage with his family in constant danger, Guy Trent becomes embroiled in moves and countermoves which may mean life or death for Western scientists.